WOMEN rent MEN and SECRETS here

Damilare Kuku is a creative artist who has worked as a radio presenter, scriptwriter, film producer and director. She holds both bachelor's and master's degrees in the Arts, hopes to start a PhD (also in the Arts) someday and maybe teach occasionally. Currently, she is an international bestselling author with books such as *Nearly All the Men in Lagos are Mad* and *Only Big Bumbum Matters Tomorrow.* Her third book is *Women Rent Men and Secrets Here*. As a child, she was drawn to the enduring magic of books and saw writers as spellcasters. Naturally, she was entranced to become one. You can follow Damilare on Instagram and X @thedamilarekuku.

Also by Damilare Kuku

Nearly All the Men in Lagos are Mad
Only Big Bumbum Matters Tomorrow

Damilare Kuku

WOMEN rent MEN and SECRETS here

London · New York · Amsterdam/Antwerp · Sydney/Melbourne · Toronto · New Delhi

First published in Great Britain by Simon & Schuster UK Ltd, 2026

1 3 5 7 9 10 8 6 4 2

Simon & Schuster UK Ltd 7th Floor,
199 Bishopsgate, London, EC2M 3TY

Simon & Schuster Australia, Sydney
Simon & Schuster India, New Delhi

www.simonandschuster.co.uk
www.simonandschuster.com.au
www.simonandschuster.co.in

The authorised representative in the EEA is Simon & Schuster Netherlands BV, Herculesplein 96, 3584 AA Utrecht, Netherlands. info@simonandschuster.nl

A CIP catalogue record for this book is available from the British Library

Paperback ISBN: 978-1-3985-2961-8
eBook ISBN: 978-1-3985-2960-1
Audio ISBN: 978-1-3985-4132-0

Typeset in Bembo by M Rules
Printed and Bound in the UK using 100% Renewable Electricity at CPI Group (UK) Ltd

My voice is bigger than me . . . .
That is why I hide it in my stories.

For J.N.,
The One who has made the voice
bigger and stronger . . .
I love you forever and a day.

Perhaps it is better to rent a man than to
 own one.
You should also rent secrets . . .
It could save you in a world that mostly
 favours those born with a third leg.

CONTENTS

MURDER

CHARACTERS

MOTIVE

PLOT TWIST

MURDER

ONE

Death of a Sugar Daddy

SATURDAY
9.15 a.m.

> A tenant has killed someone in the estate so we need to increase the rent.

Those were the words I saw on my phone's status bar after the tell-tale beep. I had been running up and down the stairs inside my flat – exercising, not being chased by demons, although one could be forgiven for thinking otherwise, since I am actively fighting writer's block. I figured that if I burned some calories while I sought inspiration for my new novel, I would be the holder of the two proverbial birds in a bush – a slim waist and a tight plot.

The message had come from the estate's WhatsApp group, and anyone who has ever belonged to one of those knows that nothing tangible is ever being said there.

Neighbours are good for either gossiping or complaining, and landlords – or managers, as they sometimes call themselves – think they've licensed your life along with the rent you've paid. They are obnoxious and nosy, in that order. So, of course, I ignored the message and continued running up and down the stairs.

It wasn't until I felt the phone vibrating and beeping like it was the end of the world that I stopped, walked to the kitchen for a drink of water, and read the rest of the message.

> We are taking this step to ensure your safety. Letters will be sent to this effect soon. We look forward to your kind cooperation.
>
> Good morning and have a blessed day.
>
> With all my love,
>
> Nicholas Ropoola,
>
> Your trusted estate manager

Leaning against the kitchen counter, I stared at my phone in disbelief. This, right here, deserves to be in the hall of fame of WhatsApp group messages. I am almost impressed. The other residents of the estate, however, are understandably vexed.

My phone repeatedly beeps in my hand. Angry words flood my screen like a swarm of bees.

You are not going to die well, sir!

What is the name of this tenant?! I just saw online that our estate is trending for murder.

I am reading the story on a blog. Her name is Juicy Mbelu!

Why are you sending this kind of a message on a Saturday? Mr Nicholas, is this a joke? You are increasing rent because a tenant killed her lover in the house?!

How did you not know she was a murderer?

Why didn't you do your background check on her?

What is this unfortunate message you sent this hot Saturday morning?

Who is this Juicy person, please?

Oh, my gawd!!! A killer in our estate? You agents will not make heaven. Only in Lagos will this happen!

> You are not well, Mr Nicholas, you want to do what? Please don't be mad!

> He has left the group. Somebody should add him back! Let me swear for that man.

I don't know if it is the thirty laps I just ran, but my knees suddenly feel weak. I head to my bedroom, once more going up the stairs, this time more contemplatively. I have just peeled off my leggings when the phone beeps again. This time it's Susan, my British literary agent. I know what she wants to say so I don't bother to read it. Instead, I click on an Instagram notification from a blogger I follow – it's a story exposing a popular broadcaster and human rights activist whose husband bullies their domestic help. A trashy read, sure, but now that I'm no longer running for inspiration, I might as well trawl the internet for the same. I'm still scanning through the post when my phone buzzes again. This time the message is from Dotun, my publicist/manager.

> Baby girl, how far? Don't you live in House Twenty-One Estate? Did you see your neighbour in the news? Click www.amebonews.com if you don't know what is happening. ALSO respond to the oyinbo woman's message, this babe. She has sent

me ten emails this week. That woman WILL find you come Nigeria.

I do not open the link.

When it comes to scandals, I prefer to maintain an anonymous distance. I value my solitude and privacy, which in Lagos is the true marker of luxury. Someone has killed someone, they want to increase rent and they have made a statement about it on a shared public platform. Only one of those three things is my problem, and it's not the first two.

In my very first Lagos apartment, the tenants saw me naked at least once a week because we all shared a toilet, kitchen and bathroom. We went from knowing each other on a first-name basis to knowing our closely held secrets. But now that I have made it to Ikoyi? I will not be so exposed again. I have lived here for eight months and my neighbours will continue to remain nameless and faceless to me, so help me God.

I ignore another message from Susan and head to the bathroom for a hot shower.

~

I have made a light breakfast, and I am sitting before my open laptop when my phone beeps again. I should really put this thing on silent. Or bury it in the potted plant by the door. In any case, I reach for it and see that the WhatsApp group has resumed posting after a brief hiatus.

> Good day All,
>
> How are we coping with this morning's news? I personally think we need to meet and discuss this rent increment. The dollar's black-market rate is now over 1200 naira. Please, I have children, some of you may be single but I have kids, so I need to save money. I suggest we meet in the garden, the one close to the generator house. Whoever is not around can reach out to me here for meeting updates.

The neighbours appear to be in the third stage of grief, seeing as they want to negotiate their way out of the bombshell hike. But anyone who lives in Lagos knows that a landlord would sooner meet his maker than reverse a rent increase. Maybe they will knock a few thousand off if they are ardent enough, but what is sure is that the amount we all paid for last year's rent is no longer an option. Still, responses come in and they unanimously agree to meet in an hour. I switch my phone to silent and place it face down on the table.

Staring at my inbox, I see a stack of emails from Susan. With a small sigh, I open the most recent one, sent minutes before she tried to call me.

Hi Ara,

I hope you are well? I haven't heard from you lately, so I just wanted to check in on how the writing is going. Are you all on track for the deadline? I'm so excited to read the new novel—

I click on the cross at the top-right of my screen, sending the reminder into oblivion.

TWO

Write or Run!

SATURDAY
2.15 p.m.

You know that suspended breath you take before your teeth sinks into the succulent flesh of an *àgbálùmọ̀*? The tension before the juice spurts, when you have no idea whether it will be sweet or sour? Whether you will end up regretting your decision to purchase the fruit just because it is in season and it brings up nostalgic childhood memories? Being a writer is exactly like that.

Every time a new story unspools from my consciousness, it exposes me to unique, multi-layered levels of torture.

First is the fervent nail chewing as I wait for feedback on the story that has lived with me for months, even years, hoping all the eyes that see it will understand the world inside my head. Then the increased heart rate as I check my email several times a day to review offers from publishers who may want to acquire the book from Susan. This stage is brutal. It feels like standing on a podium in my best dress waiting to be picked for a date. When the anxiety is unbearable, I turn to food. There's nothing on earth more soothing than a steaming hot bowl of fisherman soup and cold *eko*.

Hence all the running that I do, but I digress.

The overthinking in the first level of torture, gives way to excitement when publishers make offers to take on my manuscript, but weariness swiftly follows when the work to make it better begins. Ask any writer alive. Even when we know editing is inevitable, the process can feel like listening to other people call your child ugly and being forced to agree.

The American editor usually starts with praises, before sending three pages of notes, with an addendum that says, 'these are just suggestions', as if the choice to disregard them exists. The UK editor always appears excited by how well-written the book is, in her words – it needs no edits really – but will send two pages of notes at the last minute with a gentle reminder of the deadline. Nigerian editors are the most understanding of the language and nuance, but they often require multiple Zoom meetings to discuss the direction of the edits.

Then the final level of hell. Pub Day.

For weeks after the release, I have to pretend I am not losing my mind when the book is being dissected with the precision of a surgeon by some, and ripped apart with the viciousness of a bird of prey by others.

Here we go again. This girl is an attention whore! Writing is an art! All she does is aim for cash with her books!

Our mother is here again, and we are SAT! Ara Ikoyi can take all my savings!

Oh dear, why is this girl still a thing? I long for the days when African fiction was elusive. This babe has made reading too simple!

Finally!!! Been waiting on this for a year! Ara Ikoyi is back with another banger!

I hope you guys are happy. You have made this girl a big deal. Apparently, anyone can become a writer!

But God, I prayed to you to make this girl go away, why is she still here?! Can she just die?

Yes, Queen! She is back! Ordering for my entire community!

As much as I dislike Ara, her new book is really exceptional and well-written, better than the previous ones. I still can't stand her ass. Silly b****!

Ara Ikoyi announcing a new book has made this summer somewhat bearable. I still hate my job though!

Chinua Achebe is rolling in his grave! Wole Soyinka has gone greyer! After all the work they have done ... How is this babe the face of modern African literature? Howwwwwww??????

Please, you people should stop mentioning this commoner among literary minds! Bestselling author doesn't mean s*** to me!

And these poisonous opinions, dear heart, are just some of the demons sending me running up and down stairs, starving me of words and scenarios, wrapping like a python around my imagination.

~

I stare at the blinking cursor on my laptop screen. The work day of a person who writes for a living is disappointingly unglamorous. I spend eighty percent of my days swinging between self-hate and feeling touched by the divine, going from being unable to write a single word to not sleeping as pages and pages of words erupt out of me, but for the past eight months, I have been stuck in the former, rather than the latter.

A familiar polyphonic sound splits the silence, and moments after, the little window from WhatsApp pops up in the top right-hand corner of my screen. I look forlornly at my phone which is still lying face down. It's silent but obviously, I forgot to remove the app from my laptop.

The call is from an unfamiliar UK number. I click the green phone icon to answer it.

'Hello, Dotun. How can I help you?' I hear her distinct laugh and know I'm right.

'How did you know it was me?'

'You always go full incognito mode when I don't pick up your calls. I imagine this is another colleague's phone, or is it your new husband aiding and abetting your stalking ways?'

'My friend, keep shut! I only did that once, eight months ago, when you didn't tell me you were back in Nigeria from that book festival.' I hear her rustling something that sounds like foil before she speaks again. 'Anyway, Ara. I'm glad you are alive. I thought perhaps your neighbour killed you along with her sugar daddy.'

'I don't even know the girl. I don't know any of my neighbours. As far as I care, this estate might be occupied by ghouls—'

'See your mouth. How will you know what's going on if you never leave your house? You act like being a writer is a prison sentence. Ehn hen, while I have you, please respond to your agent. I am in the UK right now. I can't start telling the *oyinbo* woman stories because you have gone full ghost mode on your agency.'

I spin despondently on my swivel chair as if I don't know what she's talking about.

'What's happening?'

'Your fourth book, Ara! That's what is happening. Are you aware you are on a deadline? You have four months left and the *oyinbo* says you have not sent a word, let alone a chapter.' She pauses and sighs. 'You know publishing in the West is a much longer process—'

'The *oyinbo*'s name is Susan, by the way.'

'*Abeg*, rest. Answer her and do your job,' Dotun responds. 'And I hope you know that you have a book tour coming up in February next year?' she adds.

Fuck.

'Tour?'

'Yes. You know? That thing authors do where they attend events to meet their loyal readers and talk about the books they have written? Which in your case is three books? You can read excerpts from book four too, to boost preorders. It's been slated, so please submit your manuscript—'

' . . . but I have not written anything . . . ' I mutter.

I hear her sharp intake of breath. In the background, a child – probably her daughter, Funmi – screams, 'Mummy, I have finished. Please come and clean my bumbum!'

'And I didn't click that amebo link you sent me either. I don't need stark reality messing with my mojo right now. Not when I'm battling a block as big as Mount Everest,' I say to fill the silence, hoping that if I make light of what is actually heavy, she will take the hint and let me be.

She doesn't.

'Ara, listen to me. There's no such thing as writer's block. You are the writer and the block. Get out of your own way and things will flow. As a matter of fact, leave that house from time to time. Susan is on pins and needles, and I am too fine to die of stress. Write the book. Respond to Susan. God has blessed you. Don't mess it up!' She hangs up.

I fall back on the headrest, spinning slowly, staring at the ceiling, tracing the swirling POP pattern with my eyes.

THREE

Midnight Craze

SUNDAY

12.15 a.m.

By the time the heat and uneven snoring becomes unbearable, waking me up, it is midnight. The power has gone out, taking the air-con with it. Sweat has beaded around my neck and I slide out of bed to force the bedroom window open, waiting for the breeze to dry my skin. I follow the pale light of the moon as it falls like a highlighter pen on the form in my bed. His goatee, so well-groomed when he stepped into my flat four hours ago, is messy. A single droplet of sweat snakes from his forehead, down his nose and sits on his heavy upper lip. Every ten seconds or so, a different note erupts from his snoring, open mouth.

How would he look if he was dead? I wonder out of the blue.

Would he struggle if I force a pillow over his face?

What if I also take my own life afterwards? Just imagine the newspaper headlines.

HOUSE OF REP MEMBER FOUND DEAD IN WRITER'S BED.

POLITICIAN FOUND DEAD IN GIRLFRIEND'S HOME.

TWO FOUND DEAD IN APPARENT MURDER–SUICIDE IN LAGOS ISLAND.

Online bloggers, accustomed to chasing engagement coins, would editorialise and sensationalise the story, truth and forensics be damned:

> Two Bodies Found Chopped up in Bed, with the Breasts, Eyes and Private Parts Missing. One Has Been Identified as a Politician and the Other a Popular Writer.

Ah.

These must be what psychologists call intrusive thoughts. Either that or there's a spirit in House Twenty-One Estate making people want to kill each other.

In that moment, as air filters in through the open window, I know it is not murder that calls to me, but finality. It is time, at last, to end this farce of a relationship.

I send a text to Eda, my carpenter, asking him to change the locks as soon as possible.

FOUR

Lagos Rent

SUNDAY

10.18 a.m.

Ring ring.

The buzzing doorbell feels like a saw against my subconscious. I burrow my head under my pillow and throw the duvet over it, but the person pressing the button is tougher than my determination to ignore them. After two minutes of incessant ringing, I finally give up and go downstairs.

At the door, I make a futile attempt to smooth my unruly hair using the chrome flower vase as a mirror. Then I peep through the hole.

'Who is it?'

'Hi, I'm Victoria. We have not officially met, even though you moved here in January. I am your neighbour and the estate facility manager. I oversee the small, small activities in the estate when Mr Nicholas is unavailable.'

I lean against the door without opening it. 'How can I help you?'

'I don't know if you have seen the ongoing discussion in the WhatsApp group chat?'

'I have.'

'So, you should come out! I am knocking on everyone's door to place a gentle reminder.'

I look through the peephole again. She looks more irritated than she sounds, judging by how viciously she's twisting her lips, which are cartoonishly big, and painted blood red. There is a solid eight inches of door between us, but the vibes I'm picking up tell me that this woman is going to be annoying.

She continues, 'We just want to have another brief meeting about the rent increase. It's in ten minutes. In the garden!'

What part of the fact that I missed yesterday's meeting does this lady not understand? Where are we as a society if we have lost the simple art of taking a hint?

One dead sugar daddy and my carefully maintained anonymity is destroyed. Now, I have a busybody neighbour with balloon lips on my case.

Thank you, Juicy! Thanks for nothing!

I force some enthusiasm into my voice.

'Alright. See you in ten minutes.'

~

The garden is at the end of a single narrow road lined with the estate's fully detached duplexes. They all have identical blue aluminium roofs, and each house is shielded by big neem trees. The only structures that stand out are the ones that have been recently painted, the rest are like wilted onions. The estate has another garden at the other end of the road, but that one serves more as a playground since it isn't beside the generator. Unlike most estates in Lagos, there are no attached boys' quarters – only the gateman's room on the side of the main gate.

Once I get to the garden, I quickly find a seat far away from Rude Victoria. She spots me right away and pats the empty chair next to her.

'Oh, it's okay. I am fine here. Thank you!' I trill with a voice unlike mine.

Other tenants throng in after I sit down, their loud murmurs competing with the whir of the nearby water pump.

'Why would anyone increase the rent when a tenant commits murder? Are they not supposed to reduce the rent?'

'Naira is so bad, and I don't earn in any other currency so this fucking useless—'

'Shhh, there are kids here!'

'So, should I not speak freely? Why not leave your children at home?'

They find seats to perch on across the garden, their

voices getting louder. Rude Victoria jumps up, as if their complaints had wound up a coil inside her. 'Good morning, everyone. Thank you for coming, please let us wait in silence for others to join us!'

They ignore her but the harmonious murmurs descend an octave lower.

I may have been strong-armed here by Rude Victoria, but attending this meeting doesn't change my belief that this is an exercise in futility and that the neighbours sound like a broken record. Bored, I pull out my phone and check my social media, something I usually don't do when I'm trying to write . . . for obvious reasons.

As the noise drones on around me, I see that my third book, recently released in the Western – and some parts of the Eastern – hemisphere, is trending again in Lagos. People are quoting lines from it, and I see a few threads dissecting the theme and plot – mostly positively. The unexpected validation hits me like a drug, swirling around my chest. As I scroll, a popular influencer's review catches my eye:

'Ara's novels and stories capture a snapshot of contemporary Nigerian society in all its gory, raw beauty.'

I snap my phone shut as the words percolate in my head.

Dotun was right. How can I write about society when I shun it, shut myself away, avoid it? And for what? Because not everyone likes what I have to say or how I say it?

I swat a fly away and follow its escape route to the shoulder of the woman two seats away, her blue dress blending with the upholstery of the chair she's sitting on.

Rude Victoria claps her hands.

'Let us say a quick prayer.' She smiles. 'Our Father in heaven, we thank you for today. We thank you for keeping us alive and not letting us be victims of the murderer in our midst. Jesus, we have come to report our estate manager to you. In fact, all the estate managers in Lagos. God, please punish them. Bless us but punish them. Continue to uplift us. Let this meeting end in praise in Jesus's name. Amen?' she queries, as if the prayer is an instruction.

'AMEN!' some respond.

'I like your gown,' a woman in a blue burqa sitting to my left whispers to me.

'Thank you,' I whisper back.

'Please can I have your attention?' Rude Victoria's voice is piercing as an arrow. 'Are we going to pay the rent increase?' she asks like the head of a student union, looking at us to gauge our expressions.

'No!' the women chant as one.

I look around the crowd once more, paying close attention to their heads. Most of the wigs on display are worth over a million naira a piece. Why are they here debating whether they should shell out extra cash to ensure they are not homeless? Let's say we were in Ogbomosho, my mother's hometown a mere three hours away, a death in the vicinity would play out differently. Everyone would panic that they had been living in a compound with a murderer, then break into smaller groups to gossip. Some neighbours would express concern about the murder victim and others would wonder how a woman could commit such a heinous act. But here, in House Twenty-One Estate, Juicy choosing to kill her lover is more of a financial inconvenience than anything else.

Yes, I know I said I didn't care about the death or the murderer, but at least I'm not here crowing about rent instead of caring about wasted life.

'Is nobody even going to check on the girl?' someone from the other end of the garden asks. I stretch my neck to study the speaker properly. She has her hair packed in a doughnut bun, a dusting of what could be freckles or warts across her face.

A matronly woman with a small boy on her lap bellows, 'Whatever *she* has done is not any of our business. Please, if she has parents, they can sort her out. Let us focus on the rent matter. God will help the girl.'

Wait a minute. Are all the tenants in this estate women?

I do a quick headcount: there are seventeen of us here, aside from the children whose restlessness makes it impossible for me to count them all. Where are the men? Are we in a coven? How have I not noticed this before?

Someone at the back says, 'I know the girl, and I think I recognise the man she killed. He used to come here a lot.'

'Is it not that girl that has plenty of hair? Very fine girl—'

Rude Victoria cuts in. 'Please! If you want to find out about Juicy and her story, you can go and visit her! My dear sisters, we are gathered here to talk about the rent! Do you want to sleep on the road by next year? No? So, let's stick to the point!' she snarls at all of us. 'Go and see Juicy, if you are eager to be a good Samaritan. She is in custody somewhere!'

As she proceeds to describe her plans to have the estate manager arrested and thrown into Kirikiri prison, something happens to my brain.

Maybe it is the fresh air that I have been deprived of for months.

Maybe it is Dotun's advice about writer's block.

Maybe it's even the influencer's review of my work.

But at that moment, a ceiling in my head breaks open and I know I have the plot for book number four. I swear I even hear the hallelujah chorus, the realisation is that momentous.

Thank you, Rude Victoria, for the wake-up call, literally.

~

I endure twenty more minutes of diatribes, with no plan of action in view, before the force to write propels me to my feet.

'Erm, House Five, where are you going?'

See what I'm saying? This woman is mannerless. Do I look like a house to her?

'My porridge beans. The timer went off.' I wave my smartwatch. 'I have to go.'

She looks at me like I'm a flying cockroach. 'Don't you have a chef? They are not that expensive!'

See me see trouble. This woman hustling for lower rent is trying to make me feel poor.

The smile on my lips doesn't meet my eyes. 'No, I don't. I can cook my own food.'

I hear someone chuckle. *Good.* I guess some of my neighbours have a sense of humour. Rude Victoria's painted brows curl into a frown.

'Okay. If you don't come back, we will come to you—' she says.

'Or you can just leave the updates on WhatsApp,' I cut in. I hear another chuckle, louder this time. I don't wait for more distractions. I head back to my house with a spring in my step and a mission in my heart.

Who is this Juicy babe? How do I get to her? And what should I wear to a police station?

I look online for any reports of Juicy's location. Many articles spring up but two statements stand out to me – her alma mater – University of Lagos – has come out to disown her, and she is being held at Mafoluku Police Station.

What is she doing in Mafoluku? Didn't she kill her sugar

daddy here in Ikoyi? Who has the connections to get me into the cell so I can have a chat with her?

Wait a minute.

Didn't I just break up with a politician?

FIVE

Small Girl, Big Connections

SUNDAY
3.40 p.m.

Yele is speechless. The silence stretches from my ear, through eternity, and to his robust mouth. I feel like his lips are cracked open, and he might have glitched like a computer with a shitty hard drive.

'You have some fucking audacity, Ara. You broke up with me just this morning, out of the blue, the minute I woke up, for the umpteenth time! Now you want me to call the police station for you? So, you can see your neighbour that killed her benefactor?!'

He is vexed.

'Sweetheart,' I say in a voice as pliable as bubblegum. 'What we had was amazing . . . and we parted with great sex. I just need to do this.' I think of a way to appeal to his ego. 'They are threatening to triple our rent because of this murder. I need to talk to her, so I can find out if she really did it. Otherwise I might be homeless soon. Please now.'

He asks, his voice mellow, 'What if I knew the guy? What if he was my friend?'

'If you did, then I am sorry for your loss,' I say, my bubblegum voice shelved.

He chuckles. 'This girl! You are not okay at all. Now I know how you are able to write all your books.'

'Yele, please just help me. Big daddy, please.'

'You know I love you,' he coos. I roll my eyes. He whispers, 'Do you love me?'

'Yele, which one is love now?'

'Ara, just lie to me, please. Please tell me you love me.'

Darn it.

I mutter, 'I love you.'

He clears his throat and laughs. 'I'll make some calls, and you can go in on Monday.'

'Not today?'

'No. Not today. I'll need to speak to the police commissioner, who will connect me to the deputy police officer of that division, then I'll let you know.'

'Thank you. Yele, quick question. Since you have been coming here, did you notice that all the residents are women?'

'No. Are you sure? I'm sure that I have seen men in the estate.'

'I mean, the actual residents are all women.'

He laughs. 'Really? Is that not good? Girl power now. Women are making money now o. Besides, they are easier tenants. All my female tenants don't like to owe me. The men on the other hand will owe and still take you to court.'

'Hmmm.'

He adds, 'What are you doing later?'

What is wrong with this man? Does he not have work? How is a legislator so blatantly idle?

'I have to write.'

'*Oya*, write. My superstar writer. I'll sort the issue out. I am going with the President to Washington next week for a closed-door deliberation—'

'On what? How to make the country more broken and corrupt?'

'Keep shut! We are doing our best. We can't undo all the damage that was done before they gave birth to you or me.'

'Of course. Thank you so much. I'll go to the police station on Monday.'

'Love you, baby.'

I end the call.

Yele of all people should be grateful we are not together anymore. With the spirits in the air, he could easily have ended up dead.

SIX

House Visit

SUNDAY

7.30 p.m.

I am sitting before my computer outlining the plot of the novel. It is the first time in months that the four walls of this house are not a witness to me running up and down the stairs in sports gear. I have typed out just five words:

Motive. Murder. Characters. Plot Twist.

As I am chewing on my lower lip, staring at the blinking cursor, the doorbell buzzes.

I can't believe it. Does Rude Victoria have nothing else to do in life? If this whole Juicy thing didn't happen, what would she have done for fun? *Abi* is she unemployed?

This time, I don't ignore her. She won't leave anyway, and since her earlier intervention gave my writing a boost, I might as well indulge her.

I walk to the door and look through the peephole. Her

voluminous lips are all I see, but this time, the red lipstick has been replaced with a plum one. How has no one ever told her that she needs to line her lips if they are this thick and she wants to wear bold colours?

'Yes?'

'Sis, we have come to give you a summary of our meeting. Since beans is more important to you than rent.'

We? I ignore her jibe and look again to see women lined up behind her like a queue to use the ATM. I catch a glimpse of the woman in the electric blue burqa that I had seen earlier.

'Aunty, open the door now.' Rude Victoria's voice interrupts my thoughts. *Of course, she is getting impatient.* Petty me would have made her wait but the other women don't deserve to suffer for her insolence.

I open the door.

~

'Is it me or are we only women tenants here?'

Burqa voices the same thoughts I had earlier as she picks up another piece of *asun* with a toothpick. It disappears under the flap that covers the lower half of her face in a way that is both dainty and bizarre, like watching a bird of prey swallow a morsel of food.

The women have been in my house for an hour. An hour o. And they have turned me into a waitress in my own home. Thankfully I shop in bulk and in variety, so I have enough snacks for everyone. Even pre-cooked, frozen *asun*.

A woman in a blue denim jacket and black jeans responds to Burqa. 'It is not just you. I noticed this about a year ago. Every tenant is a single mother, a spinster or recently divorced.'

Rude Victoria holds up a cushion in her hand, inspecting it. 'This your house is nice o, Sis. What do you do?'

'I write.'

'Ehn? Like, what is your real job?'

'She just told you,' another woman in a thin-strapped pink maxi dress answers. Beside her is a lady in boubou who is silent, but her eyes follow the gaggle of children as they run around. Her legs are impressively long. From where she sits on my sofa, they nearly touch the coffee table.

'What kind of writing allows you to buy a sofa worth over two million naira?' She runs her hand across the surface. 'I recognise this brand from Vento. Are you like those useless bloggers that ruin people's lives with their gossip?'

'I'm an author.'

She twists her lips to the side in disbelief. 'Or do you have a big man somewhere, sustaining your lifestyle?'

Obviously, these women don't read. How do they plan to raise their children? With advice from influencers on TikTok or Instagram?

Mid last year, my third novel – plotted around how a

divisive presidential election broke up many Nigerian families, eventually leading to a civil war – was released. Last month, Susan sent an email to say that international and local sales were stronger than for my previous two books together. Yet here I am in my living room being accused, however subtly, of being a prostitute by my neighbour.

'Let it go, Victoria,' interjects the robust woman whose laps her child has finally escaped, revealing her hairy legs in the process.

Without taking her eyes off me, Rude Victoria presses. 'What have you written? Maybe I have seen it?'

A woman in an *ankara iro* and *buba*, a small scarf around her head, shifts the subject.

'Let's leave work aside. Who is that girl, Juicy?'

'Those small, small Lagos girls that go around snatching people's husbands, of course. God finally caught her,' Rude Victoria, full of bile, responds.

'But was she friends with anyone in the estate?' I ask.

Rude Victoria raises her voice. 'You people! That is enough about this girl. I really don't understand why we are not all happy that we have been rid of a sugar daddy-killer. Rent is the focus. Maybe Ms Writer can help us sell her sofa to cover the increase. Until then, Ms Writer, we have decided to give Mr Nicholas three days to turn on his phone before we have another meeting.'

That's her grand plan? To threaten the landlord to turn on

his phone? Two meetings to achieve this, just to walk into my home and throw jibes at me?

Irritated, I get up and stack their plates one on top of the other, the clattering sounds soothing. As I head to the kitchen, I hear an argument between the women brewing. By the time I set the plates down in the sink, their voices are raised, so I rush back into the living room.

'Are you trying to insinuate that all of us are *ashewos* in Lagos?!' Rude Victoria is now screaming at Burqa.

'No. I am saying women have always been seen as sex objects by most Nigerian men. Some are just smart enough to cash in on it.'

Wow, Burqa is brutal!

'I am not a prostitute. I am a woman of virtue. A child of God.' Rude Victoria looks like she is ready to kill Burqa.

'Hallelujah!' Burqa exclaims.

'Let's go and leave the poor writer alone,' Long Legs says.

The writer in me immediately interjects.

'Please, don't leave. Would you like some hibiscus tea and ginger? I made it yesterday with lots of date powder. Very cold.'

Rude Victoria may be annoying, but my brain cells clearly crave the antagonism.

I serve them tumblers of the ice tea as they share stories about the estate manager and how he finds ways to scam the tenants. Soon, they are talking about landlords as a whole category of crime in Lagos.

'It's almost as if these people want to punish us for daring to have a better life. One of my friends says the service charge for her apartment is close to three million naira and her rent is eight million.'

'That is nothing. You know that Belmonte apartment on Alexander Ikoyi? Rent there is a hundred thousand dollars per year. Why are you charging Nigerians in their own country in foreign currency?!'

'This is why girls like Juicy need sugar daddies,' Rude Victoria exclaims triumphantly.

Wow. This woman never lets go!

After another hour, they finally return to their houses. I spend some time cleaning downstairs before I start to plot the movements for my next story in my head. I return to my laptop, open another document and write down my next steps:

- Take a taxi to Mafoluku Police Station on Monday.
- Speak to Yele's DPO contact.
- Interview Juicy for a few hours.
- Come home and start writing a book about her.
- Submit the first draft of the book within six months.
- Get Susan and Dotun off my back.

This should be easy.

SEVEN

Who is Juicy?

SUNDAY

10.20 p.m.

I can't sleep, so I trawl social media, looking for any new information on Juicy. I enter her name into the Instagram search bar, but her personal account is private, with few followers, giving little away. Her bio reads: *Jesus baby/Dreamer.*

I type #Juicythesugardaddykiller into the search bar and find a glut of videos where she is the main character.

The first recording is dimly lit by a red light. In it, Juicy is dancing with three girls clad in lacy lingerie. Olamide's 'Pawon' plays in the background. A few seconds later, she walks to the pole in the centre of the room and starts to whine her waist. Her focus is on whoever is recording the video. She wags her index finger at the camera, blows kisses, and then wads of naira shower all over her. As the torrent of money increases, the other dancers join Juicy at the pole, picking up the cash, while Juicy continues to dance enticingly. The shot ends with Juicy laughing as she is pulled in by whoever is filming.

Another video opens with Juicy asleep in bed. The camera slowly pans up from her feet, with the white sheets in between her legs, stopping at the top of the red lace panties just below her navel.

'Wake up, baby. I want to eat you,' a croaky voice says, then the camera moves quickly to her face. Juicy does not budge, then a hairy hand taps her shoulder, and she drowsily opens her eyes. She is smiling, but her expression changes to panic when she sees the lens.

'My love, why are you recording me while I am sleeping?'

'I want evidence that someone like me can have a beautiful girlfriend like you. I am going to use you to win points with the boys.'

She smiles. 'Sweetheart, you can't play this for anyone. I am naked.'

The voice challenges her. 'Why? Is everyone not naked now?' She laughs at the comment and draws the sheets up to cover her body. 'I don't know anyone who looks this good in the morning,' the voice continues.

'Aww. Baby, put the camera away, please. I am not properly dressed.'

'Okay, if you promise to give me some Juice.'

She rolls away from the camera and the voice laughs at her discomfort.

In another video that has over a million views, the angle shows that it is self-recorded. She looks more comfortable as she speaks directly to the camera.

'Hi, Montana, sorry I missed your call, baby girl. Your phone is not reachable, so I am leaving you a message on Snapchat. How are you, darling? I am on set to support Halima. She is shooting her video for her latest song. Please make sure to watch and stream all her songs. Tell your viewers and fans to support my girl o. *Ehn hen*, let me show you the car and bag I am rocking this Friday. It's my baby's car but what belongs to my baby is mine. The bag is mine *sha*.'

She turns the camera around to show a Bentley and a Birkin bag, both orange. She flips the camera back to her face. 'I am doing "to match".' She grins and then ends the recording.

On Facebook, an anonymous account has several videos of Juicy. In one of them, she looks younger, dressed in a raspberry-coloured bodycon dress that pushes her tiny cleavage up to her neck. She is unaware of the camera at first, but once she sees it, she smiles and says, 'We are out here hustling. Your girl is going to be a big woman someday with plenty of money that is her own. And it starts here!' The video ends abruptly as someone from behind the lens screams, 'Next!'

Another video shows her rolling a blunt with an ease that says it's not her first time. She lights it and takes a drag before she addresses the camera, 'According to the great Michelle Obama, when they go low, we go high!' She laughs at her joke. A man comes into the frame, and slings his arm across her shoulders, smiling.

'Only Juicy would quote the First Lady of America while smoking a joint!'

She smiles back at him. 'She is a classy woman. Something we all aim to be. Who do you want me to quote? The woman whose husband told the whole world she belongs in *ze* kitchen?'

They start to laugh, and the video fades out.

I am fascinated by her. Nothing about the videos I have seen indicate that she's capable of that kind of violence.

EIGHT

Kola-nut Breath and Other Mini Disasters

MONDAY

8.30 a.m.

I see the half-naked man approaching before he knocks on my window.

He winks at me, then starts to tug at the door. I am in the backseat of an Uber in bumper-to-bumper traffic. The driver, who is looking ahead, seems oblivious. So, I try to ignore him, but my heart beats so furiously in my chest, I imagine it is visible, pulsing beneath my yellow silk shirt. From behind my dark cat-eye shades, I discreetly observe the naked man. There is a pair of broken binoculars in his tangled hair, and the lower half of his face is hidden by a matted beard. A torn red T-shirt hangs loosely around his shoulders, a sack slung over it. His lower body is unclothed, and I quickly avert my eyes.

I should not have to see a stranger's penis on a Monday morning!

'*Laydee,* open the door!' the man screams. He is now drawing hearts on the window, leaving a dirty trail with his index finger. 'If you call an African woman, woman, she no go *gree*, she go sayyyy, she go say I be *laydee* o.' His cracked voice seeps through the glass that separates us.

Waiiittt. Is that Fẹlá Aníkúlápó Kúti's song, 'Lady'?

Finally, the driver looks up, trying to gauge what's going on through the rear-view mirror.

'*Oga*, please move forward!' I whisper.

'Madam, we are in lockdown. Nowhere to move.'

'Are you not scared he will spoil your car?'

'Not really, ma. The car is old, anyone that tries to spoil it will injure himself.' The words draw lazily from his lips like okro soup.

The driver and I are now trapped watching the obscene theatre of the half-naked man dancing to accompany his singing.

'*Na* me go marry you *eh eh*, I suppose to marry you *ay ay*.'

Now he's singing a Zakki Azzay tune. *What will I do if this man succeeds in opening the door?* I inch towards the other side of the car to create more space between us. Suddenly the traffic moves, and the tooting cars behind force the driver to accelerate quickly, leaving the man in the dust. I give in to the temptation to look back, only to see that he is giving energetic chase.

This can only happen in Lagos.

Thankfully, the car gathers more speed and soon we are on the expressway.

'Madam, do you have a preferred route?' the driver inquires.

'No, sir.' I lean into my seat with a smile. 'Why don't we just follow the map?'

'Madam, the map is not always correct. Are we going to the police station in Mafoluku?'

'Yes.'

He squints at me in the mirror. 'Are you a criminal or do you want to go report somebody?'

'I am a criminal, *oga*. Now, please focus on the road.'

Chastened, he takes a turn to get onto Eko Bridge, and I can finally relax. I take in the old buildings on an unnamed street, and the passers-by who have only their hands to shield them from the merciless early morning sun.

But my peace does not last.

'Madam, should we take the right, left or middle road once we come down from the bridge?' the driver asks again.

'*Oga*, I am not familiar with this area. I don't know Oshòdì well. I really think our best bet is the map.'

He laughs. 'So why are you going to the police station in a place you don't know? Why not go to Lekki Police Station?'

'Please can you just follow the map?'

He mimics my tone. 'I too am not familiar with the map so we will both get lost.'

I roll my eyes. *Shebi, if I had just followed the map and driven my car, I would have avoided all this?*

I say nothing as my attention shifts to the commotion outside at a farmer's market. A woman selling golden melons is on her knees, counting her cash, the fruit stacked beside her. Her feet, which are a deep red from the dust, contrast with her sallow face and pink lips – that are no doubt chemically enhanced. Around the corner, a famished-looking man in a three-piece suit drenched in sweat is selling thrift blazers. Every face I see looks tired of the daily hustle and bustle. And the day has barely started.

~

'We *aff reach* the station, madam.' The Uber driver's kola-nut breath hits my face, waking me.

To avoid the rancid smell that immediately assails my senses, I duck my head, nearly bumping my nose against his before he draws back slightly. '*Oga*, why are you speaking directly into my face?!'

He smiles. 'I have been calling you. You were dozing under your glasses, so I wanted to check that you were not dead. I have carried passengers who died before. It is not my portion again. Monday morning palaver is not the will of Ogun for me.'

I slide past him and get out of the car, walking towards the station. It suddenly occurs to me to stop and search my bag to be sure I have not been robbed. *Phew. My things are intact.*

'*Shioor* not every Uber driver is a thief! Stupid girl. Common criminal,' he yells.

I look back and find him leaning against his car, watching me. I hurry away before he disgraces my ancestors, finding myself before the station; a green building with a large sign over the entrance to my far right.

A painted print on the metal signboard reads:

MAFOLUKU POLICE STATION.
Police is your friend.
Please come in.

Inside the building, I stroll past a crowd of bus drivers yelling at each other, even though there is an officer in their midst. Looking beyond the fracas, I try to find a friendly face to help me.

'Yes!' A woman in uniform appears from nowhere and stops me with both hands before I reach the counter.

'Good afternoon, ma. I am here to see the DPO on behalf of Senator Yele Onechance.'

She drops her hands immediately, and smiles. 'Ah, sorry. I didn't know you were an important person, madam. Please, follow me.'

Typical.

I follow her as she heads off past the counter and down a long corridor with the holding cells on either side. The officer escorts me into a narrow office at the end, and ushers me into a plastic chair opposite the DPO, who is rounding off a phone call. His hairline is the first thing I notice. Clearly balding, he and his barber have nonetheless entered into a conspiracy to disguise the fact, creating a false hairline with dye and contouring. But anyone with eyes can see the lie.

Once the DPO puts down the telephone, the officer who brought me in introduces me: 'This is the madam from the senator, sir.'

The DPO opens his arms. 'Madam, you are welcome! *Oga* Yele has told me everything. You want to see Juicy?'

I take my shades off, and his smile broadens at the gesture.

'Yes, sir.'

I move to place my bag on the desk, but when I notice a patch of dried locust beans stuck to the area in front of me, I keep my bag on my lap. A sweet smell of freshly baked bread comes through the windows, and I smile.

Freshly baked Agege Bread is life.

The DPO watches me closely. 'Come o. Are you her sister? See as both of you fine!' He rubs his hands together. I immediately regret taking my shades off. He wouldn't have been so familiar otherwise.

'No, sir.'

He stops smiling. 'Who are you then? Is that girl an orphan? You are the first person to come and visit her since she has been here.'

'Can I see her now?'

His eyes travel all over me. Lingering on my mouth, he smacks his dry lips like I am a bowl of *efo riro* he's been craving. I sit patiently, ignoring the urge to lean over and slap his greasy head. After he is done eyeballing me, he drags out his next words.

'Let one of my officers go and call her.' We sit in silence as the female officer goes to summon Juicy. He steals further glances at me. 'You are a beautiful woman, ma.'

I keep the smile plastered across my face. 'Thank you.'

I am no mind-reader, but I can bet my assets that there's only two thoughts bouncing around that contoured head of his: whether or not I am Yele's woman, and how much money he would need to have to be able to fuck me, if not.

The officer quickly returns. 'I am sorry, *sah*. She say she no *dey* expect anybody.'

The DPO shakes his head furiously. 'That girl is too stubborn. Since she come station on Friday, she no *gree* talk to anyone,' he says.

Strange. In my frenzied research last night, I read dozens of articles with interviews purported to be conducted with Juicy. Does this mean no one, no family or even the press has come to verify the allegations?

'Even when the wife of the *Oga wey she kpai dey* bite all over her body, she no i talk. She just *dey* silent, *dey* cry,' the DPO explains further.

'Has she eaten since she got here?' I ask.

He scratches his head. 'No.'

Three days without food. I can't say I blame her. Except for the brief aroma of the sweet scent of fresh bread, there is a persistent gross odour oozing from the inner corridors into the office that mingles with the smell from the gutters just outside the station. The noisy air conditioner unit in the corner of this office only helps to spread the mixture of unholy smells.

No one should eat anything here.

'Madam, we are sorry. Please, help us tell *Oga* sorry. You can't see her.'

I smile sweetly at the DPO. 'I have to see her.'

'Madam, the person *wey* bring her here say make we no force her talk and *na* top *Oga*. Until she is ready to talk, we have instructions not to touch her.'

Juicy, you are going to have to talk to me. You are the main character of my next book, and they have paid me the advance, so we are in this together.

I fish in my bag for the stuffed envelope that I brought as a backup in case Yele's influence was not enough.

'Let me talk to you alone, sir,' I say. He uses his eyes to signal the other officer away. I put the envelope on the table, my fingers lingering over it as I instruct him.

'I need to see her. I'm sure you can make it happen.' I lift the flap of the envelope. He sees the dollar notes and the lip smacking begins again. He is breathing like he's running up a vertical incline, and he taps the side of his head before speaking again.

'We really can't force her, but we can use her lawyer. She talks to that one. He came in yesterday,' he explains.

I inch the envelope closer to him and his eyes follow the movement hungrily.

'Come back the day after tomorrow. She will talk.' He reaches for the envelope with filthy nails.

'Please, don't manhandle her. I just want to speak to her,' I add as I slide the envelope closer to him, making sure to avoid our hands touching.

'Madam, please don't tell us how to do our job!' he retorts, but his eyes stay on the envelope. I withdraw my hand.

He licks his lips again, his tongue lingering against the lower lip before he pulls it back into his mouth. 'You can come at ten in the morning, on Wednesday.'

'Thank you.' I lean forward so my breasts can distract him from paying attention to my next request. 'I will probably come every day after to see her since she has no one else. Is that okay, *sah*?' The distraction works. His gaze locks on my bosom.

'Are you a journalist? What do you want with her?'

'I am her friend from school.'

'Then you are her sister! That way you can come as many times as you like. Just come by ten and leave by twelve. The wife of the dead man comes at two in the afternoon to cry for justice,' he advises, then slips the envelope under his desk.

~

Once I get home, I take a deeper dive into Njoku Onaogu, Juicy's sugar daddy. Most articles about the case focus more on Juicy than him. The internet offers very little information, the key takeaway being that he was the CEO of Maynard Communications, a telecommunications company and one of the major sponsors of the Big Brother franchise. From what I have seen, Juicy must have been affiliated in some way with the show, since most of her friends on social media were alums.

I scoff as I read. I have always hated that awful reality show. I have no idea what people find so entertaining in it. No. I take that back. Watching adults pretending that they don't see a camera watching them finger fuck each other is laughable.

Moving on, another report I find suggests that there was no way she was living in House Twenty-One all alone, alleging that most sugar babies in Lagos move in packs. I file that away in the folder of questions I plan to ask when I see her.

Another blog, *Gossip Lover*, delved into her past. Born in

Ajegunle, and an only child, Juicy's beauty made her popular so quickly that it was almost inevitable that she wound up as a sugar baby. This report also claims she is a final year Mass Communications student at Unilag.

In one Twitter thread, a journalist wrote that the day before she killed her sugar daddy, Njoku, she had been partying hard on a yacht. The tweets went on to describe how, during the exchange, she stabbed him multiple times and then sliced him up. The blurred images attached to the thread show her next to chopped-off chunks of what I can only assume are the deceased.

Another influencer wrote that Juicy is five foot four and Njoku over six foot tall.

How could this tiny, timid-looking girl kill this man?

I pull up pictures of him with his wife, the so-called biter – according to the DPO. They have three children together – all boys. I attempt to check his Instagram page, but it has been deactivated.

The wife's page is easier to access. On closer inspection, I see that she looks like an older version of Juicy, with tiny lines etched on her face that I am sure her husband's cheating ways put there. I look through pictures of her taken in the years before motherhood made her curvier.

Yup. Definitely a carbon copy of Juicy.

Restless Nation gives more information about the incident, saying that after their day on the yacht, Juicy and Njoku had both smoked marijuana and he was trying to initiate sexual relations when they had a quarrel. Then she killed him.

This story does not add up abeg.

On Snapchat, there's a viral video of her recorded the night before, confirming the yacht story. In it she is vaping, twerking with some girls on a boat. A pot-bellied silhouette frequently casts a shadow over their dancing figures. Njoku was lean and fit. So, who was she on the yacht with? Maybe this is why they had a fight?

I zoom into the video and recognise one of the girls. It's Montana Monaco. This must be the Montana she was addressing in one of those earlier videos. She presents a TV show on Channel 141, in which influential Nigerian figures share their success stories. I go to her page. Her posts show that she too is a student at the University of Lagos, studying for a master's degree in Mass Communication.

Well, it looks like I'm going back to university in the morning.

NINE

Field Research

TUESDAY
7 a.m.

Warm rays of sunlight wake me up. Still drowsy, I check my phone. I have to be at the University of Lagos in two hours. But first, I am going to make a quick stop at the house next door. Perhaps the woman living there will have something on Juicy that will help me as I start to write.

I inspect my look once more before I step out to knock on the door of the next duplex, which is just five feet away from mine.

'It's open,' a deep, throaty voice answers. Is there a male tenant in the estate? I push at the security door, and it gives way quite easily. Are these people just leaving their homes open? Yes, we live in Ikoyi – inarguably the most affluent neighbourhood in the city – but this is still Lagos. Daylight robbery is a real battle, not a myth.

'Hi. It's Ara, your neighbour,' I say, before entering.

'I know, I can see you.'

Oh. I look around and spot a tiny camera attached to the door frame.

'Come in, I am upstairs in the bathroom.'

'I can come back another time.'

'No . . . it's fine, just follow my voice.'

There is an arrow on the brown hardwood floor that signals the way upstairs. The dark orange walls feel ominous, but I follow the arrows up the staircase, unsure of where to go next.

'Just turn left, and then right,' she guides me. How does she know where I am? 'I can tell you're flat-footed from the way you walk. Just follow my voice,' she adds.

A minute later, I am in her bedroom, an exotic den lined with leopard-print wallpaper.

Wait, Long Legs is my neighbour?

There are pictures of her everywhere, with people I assume are family. Her voice still guides me, even though I don't need it. I can now see that the layout of her house is an exact replica of mine.

'You can come in,' she says.

'I don't mind waiting for you to be done.'

'Come in!'

'Okay.' I turn towards the bathroom and open the door. Inside, the air is warm and humid, the scent in the air like a bouquet of roses. The walls and floor are tiled in gold, and the cup-like tub she sits in is deep bronze.

Her right leg hangs loosely over the tub's edge, and water drips from her elegant toes onto the bathmat.

Why is this woman okay being naked with a stranger in her bathroom?!

I shift my gaze to her face, and meet her eyebrows quizzically arched. 'We met on Saturday,' I explain.

She turns her attention to her right leg, watching as the water drips. Meanwhile, I am fighting the urge to shove the leg back into the tub.

'Yes, I remember. You're the writer,' she responds.

'I am. My name is Ara. I realise we didn't introduce ourselves properly that day.'

'Names are unimportant. We are neighbours, not friends.'

'Okay . . . ' I am not sure how to approach the subject now that she has set a somewhat unfriendly tone, despite inviting me into her bathroom.

'Are you here to discuss the rent increase?' she asks.

'I wanted to ask if you knew Juicy. I figured someone here must have known her.'

'Yes, I did. We became friends when she moved here,' she replies, folding her right leg back into the tub.

Oh wow!

She points to a small plastic white chair next to the bath. 'Sit.'

There is an awkward silence as I watch her start to rinse her body. I look down at my fingers and fiddle with the strap of my bag, waiting.

After a few minutes, she asks, 'Why do you want to know about Juicy?'

'I'm just curious.'

She looks at me. 'Curious or nosy?' She smiles and continues, 'My dear, that girl nearly snatched my boyfriend. When she moved in, all I wanted was to be a big sister to her. We became close, then she met my man. She told me a month later he was toasting her. I chased her away and ended the friendship.'

So, Juicy got the boot, not the man who was pursuing his woman's friend? Interesting.

She steps out of the tub. 'Girls like that are like slow poison.'

Ha. This woman is casually walking around naked before someone she doesn't even know. Is this the twilight zone? *Abi* Lagos had dialled up the insane without me noticing? She resumes speaking as she walks towards the towel rack.

'Juicy is a good girl. She is not troublesome. It's just that her beauty makes men foolish. This is why no one has gone to visit her. She probably snatched all her other friends' men.'

I stand. 'Thank you for talking with me. I should head out.'

She stops mid-stride and turns. 'Leave Juicy's matter alone. She will be fine.'

'Of course. Thank you.'

I walk out of her house, get into my car and head to the University of Lagos.

~

The heat of the mid-morning sun stings my arms through the rolled-up windows as I approach the University of Lagos. The yellow-painted crown at the entrance appears grand, but it shrinks disappointingly the closer I get. There are two gates at the entrance that lead in and out of the campus. As I drive in through the gate on the right, a man in a blue uniform gives me a metal card.

'Good afternoon, madam,' he says.

'Good afternoon, *sah*,' I respond. 'Please, I am going to the Department of Mass Communication.'

He points ahead. 'Just keep driving straight. After two roundabouts, you will reach a fire station, and it is the building opposite—' Cars start to honk at us.

Nigerians and their inherent rush to go nowhere.

The man turns to the driver of the vehicle behind me. '*Oga*, calm down *na*. She needs direction, so hold on.' He turns to face me. 'So, madam, go straight—'

'It's okay, sir,' I interject. 'Let me find a place to park here so you can take your time to describe it. I am new here and don't want to get confused.'

I drive to a spot just ahead and park. In my rear-view mirror, I see a mousy-looking young woman in a cyan-coloured midi dress, her hair tucked under a scarf, approaching my car. I don't want a repeat of Monday's madness with the half-naked man, so I raise my tinted window until it's almost shut. As anticipated, she taps on it.

'Aunty, please can I help you? I am going to campus. I can direct you anywhere. Just give me a ride.'

The security officer is now behind her. '*Ehen, abeg*, let her show you, my dear sister. She is my boss's girlfriend. She will help you find the place.' He addresses her. 'Show her Mass Comm,' and walks back to the gate.

Apparently, neither of these two care that I may be a serial killer or a suicide bomber.

The woman jumps into the car with me, and I start down the road. Out of nowhere, a bus corners us, nearly hitting the mirror on the passenger side.

'*Ashewo*!' the driver yells. 'See as you park like say *na* your papa get the road. *Werey*!'

I ignore him, slowing my pace, trying to avoid running into the speed breaker just ahead.

'*Na* your mama and papa be *ashewo*!' the mousy girl beside me shouts, taking me aback. 'You will not die well. Your entire family *na ashewo*!' She doesn't bat an eyelid afterwards, leaning back against the seat as if she wasn't the one who just spoke.

I smile to myself. It pays never to underestimate anybody in Lagos.

As we drive along, I take in the scenery of one of the country's most prestigious universities. The lanes are divided by dusty flower beds, the pavements lined with palm trees, shielding people from the harsh sun, and there are a few commercial banks. I see a bus stop with many people queuing, trying to get into buses and taxis. There is a fire station further down on the other side of the road.

The mousy lady uses her hands to direct me. 'This is Mass Communication. *Oya*, go far down.' I drive on until she says, 'Stop stop, *na* here. Drive in and park.' We go into a compound that houses the department – a grey, two-storey building. She turns to face me. 'Aunty don't do like say you are a stranger here o. They will not let you park in the department.' Then she gets out of the car, closes the door and pauses to look at me.

The gentle expression I first saw at the gate creeps back.

'Aunty, sorry that I shouted. I am pregnant and my baby is worrying me. Also, my husband has not agreed to marry me. I am not happy at all. I am a respectable secretary and worker in the Church. Out-of-wedlock child is bad. That *yeye* bus driver is not well. Why is he calling *ashewo*?'

'My dear sister, we are all *ashewos*. Some of us are just better at hiding it. Don't feel bad.'

Her expression goes from conciliatory to one of shock. She storms off, her scarf momentarily slipping off her head and she stops to fetch it.

'Yes? Hello! What do you want?' I turn and see a

heavy-set security officer in his blue uniform and beret coming towards me. Remembering Mousy's advice, I think of a clever response.

'Good afternoon. I am a visiting lecturer,' I say as soon as he gets to my car. The fire in his eyes goes out and he struggles to give a smile. 'I need to see a colleague,' I add.

'Who?'

'Dr Udenwa.' I had looked up all the lecturers before I came. The one I just mentioned is also the head of the department.

He laughs. 'That's my big madam. She is expecting you, *abi*?'

'Yes, she is.'

He backs away from the car. 'Oh, okay. Please, park well. If they hit this your fine jeep, nobody will pay you o. *Na* sorry *dey* go tell you.'

After I park properly, he takes me inside. I hear a noise as we walk down a dark and dusty corridor using the torch light from his phone to guide us.

Why is there so much shouting?

'The non-teaching staff are having a meeting in one of the halls – they want to go on strike for unpaid hazard allowances, government has been owing them for three years,' the man explains, as if he can see my curiosity. He leads me down another corridor which is better lit, though the blue walls are cracked and faded.

'You can go in.' He gestures as we reach a brown door with a nameplate that says Dr Udenwa – Head of Department.

'Thank you.'

He lingers, expecting me to go in. I smile at him, waving my phone. 'I need to make a call first.'

After he leaves, I take a deep breath and knock.

'Mrs Tinubu, enter *biko*. Where is the *Oyeil*? This Indomie is about to burn!' a voice with an unmistakable Igbo accent calls out. I walk in and a woman in a yellow peplum top, blue skirt and bathroom slippers is standing over a pot on a hot plate in the corner of the office. She turns around. It's the lecturer. I recognise her from her picture on the website. There is a 2018 calendar hanging on the wall just beside her head. Her desk is littered with papers and books and a green sofa adorns the other side of the room, opposite the makeshift kitchenette.

'Yes? Who are you?'

'Good afternoon, ma. My name is Ara.'

She turns down the flames and walks away from the pot to stand behind the desk. 'Madam, I don't see masters' students during the week. Come and find me at home on Saturday or Sunday evening. Bring your gifts for my wedding anniversary along with you. Now as you can see, I am about to have my lunch—'

'I am not a student, ma.'

She seems uncomfortable now. 'Who are you looking for?'

'You, ma.'

'Are you from the Vice Chancellor? For the—'

'No, ma. I am a journalist.'

'Oh.' She relaxes and takes a seat behind her desk. 'Are you the one from the *Restless* newspaper that wants to cover my wedding anniversary?'

'No, ma.'

She eyes me at this point.

'Please, address me as a doctor. How can I help you?' Her eyes dart to the corner where the noodles are cooking, the steam sneaking out from the pot starting to warm the already stale air in the office.

'I want to find out about a young lady called Juicy Mbelu. I understand she is your student. I am writing an article—'

'What newspaper?' she asks.

Shit. I didn't think she would ask me that. '*Arise TV News*, Doctor.' My answer somehow satisfies her, and she gets up to remove the lid from the pot.

'Ohhhhh. You people are big now. Listen, Miss, or is it Mrs?'

'Miss Ara, Doctor.'

'Ara? What kind of name is that? Why are you not married? Young fine girl like you.' She continues as if she doesn't expect an answer. '*Nne*, I can't answer questions about Juicy. She hardly ever came to class and when she did, she distracted everyone with her flamboyant lifestyle. Not a particularly bright young lady. I think she got a D in my class last semester. I have not marked their papers yet for this semester, but I'm sure she will fail. So, I am not surprised she is now in her present predicament.'

I want to tell her that academic excellence means very little in the real world, and that life favours whomever it likes. But that is not a battle I want to enter into with a lecturer.

The lecturer continues to speak. '*Bia*, Juicy is not a special girl. She is like all the harlots that stroll around on this campus lying to themselves that they are students!' She stops briefly to remove the pot of noodles from the heat. 'But I am happy to tell you about my wedding anniversary, if you can assure me of a post on social media. I will pay you fifty thousand naira, after you make the post and send me the link.'

'Okay, Doctor.' I give her my phone number, and she immediately sends me an article I assume she has written. There is a photo included, in which she and her husband sit close to one another in matching dark brown suits, looking straight into the camera. Both have worn-out looks on their faces as if the photographer had exhausted them with instructions.

I look up to see her dipping a fork into the pot and scooping the noodles into a transparent bowl. 'So, Doctor, did Juicy ever—' Another woman walks in.

The lecturer turns to me. 'This is the departmental secretary, Mrs Tinubu. You can call her Mrs T.' She turns to Mrs Tinubu. 'This is Aramanda from *Arise TV*.' She takes a forkful of noodles into her mouth, and we wait as she chews slowly. 'My dear, I don't know anything about Juicy. She killed that man and ruined a family. *Chai*, that his poor wife!'

'Please, Doctor, do you know anyone who can help me?'

She doesn't answer. The secretary smiles at me briefly to acknowledge my presence.

'Hello, sister Aramanda.'

Dr Udenwa addresses her again. '*Ehn hen*, I have been waiting for you. Indomie has burnt *sef* because no *oyeil*, but did you bring me the—' She pauses mid-sentence to look at me, smiles and her eyes swing to the door. I have been dismissed.

Outside the office, I delete her number and message, then I linger around the corridor watching students throng in and out of rooms. I try to imagine being one of them, dashing to catch classes taught by lecturers who make noodles in their offices.

Down the corridor, I see a sign that says: *University of Lagos 103.1 FM radio*, just above a red door with studio lights, and I head towards it.

'Stop there.' A high, falsetto voice stops me from opening the wooden door. 'That's a live studio! They are on air.'

I turn around to see a youngish-looking chap with tri-colour hair dressed in multi-coloured shorts, a turtleneck and a septum ring hanging loosely from his nose. He walks past me and leans against the door as though to block the entrance. 'Are you new here? Interns go downstairs to the newsroom.'

'No. I am looking for a student. A Montana Monaco.'

'A student here? Is she an intern at Unilag FM?'

'I think she is doing a postgraduate degree here.'

'Describe her.'

Does this gangly-looking fellow think of himself as a human GPS? How is he going to find someone in an over-crowded department with a mere description?

'If she is popular, I will definitely know her,' he says, reading my mind. I show him the pictures of Montana together with Juicy on my phone. He taps the screen excitedly. 'Oh, I know her and even that babe. That proud one with edges. *Na* she police just arrest. God finally caught that girl. Very proud.'

'Did you know Juicy?'

'Yes and no. No, because she never used to talk to boys on campus as if we were too small for her. Yes, because she was very popular and we took some courses together.'

I tap on Montana's picture again. 'Do you know where I can find her?'

He looks around as if Juicy and Montana might be behind

us, and then kisses his teeth before answering. 'When Juicy got arrested, I heard her friend ran off to Dubai.'

'Ran off? As in, she left Nigeria? Didn't Juicy just kill her sugar daddy last week?'

'*Ehn hen*? To go to Dubai is not hard for all these *ashewos*. She posts snaps from Dubai now.'

That word again.

You know, at this point, we have to get the national agency of orientation to educate the masses to stop using *ashewo* as a slur. But what do I know? They probably disagree, seeing that slut-shaming is a national sport across both genders. I thank him and walk towards the exit.

Heading for the stairs, I see a blue door with a nameplate that reads Dr Olorogun. I stop to decide if I should ask this lecturer for more information on Juicy. After my last encounters, I'm hesitant, but I knock anyway. The lecturer opens the door just a few inches, and I can hear the sound of a television blaring in the office behind him.

'Yes?'

'Good afternoon, sir. My name is Ara, I am from *Arise TV News*. I have a few questions about Juicy—'

'Oh my God! How many people will ask about this girl? Juicy was my student for one semester and during that time, she was rumoured to be dating one of the university's major sponsors for events organised on campus, so I avoided her. The stupid girl refused to buy any of my books. She had all that money. Please don't quote me. I don't want any trouble!'

'Okay, sir, but—'

'Are you a new student as well? Will you like to buy my books? They are instrumental—'

'I am not a student, sir—'

'Young lady, please don't disturb me.'

The door is closed in my face, and I hear a bolt sliding into place, after which the volume of the television rises to a deafening level. I head downstairs to my car.

The security guard hobbles towards me as I reverse out quickly. He throws his hands up in surrender as I zoom off.

What do I do now?

I will try Solomon, the gateman. I have given him enough money, bread and Coca-Cola to be able to gather some Juicy gist.

~

I return to the estate just after midday. The parking space allotted to House Two is empty, so I drive into it. Solomon calls out to me as he struggles to lock the estate's heavy iron gate behind me. He runs over to my car.

'Aunty Ara, you can't park there! I beg you. The woman who owns that space has reported me to the estate manager many times.'

The evening I moved into the estate, he helped to arrange

my living room furniture. After we were done moving boxes, I thanked him, and he took my invitation for snacks as a cue to tell me his life story. He has two wives and seven children in Kogi State, as well as his extended family, who all rely on him as their sole breadwinner. 'Aunty, my salary does not reach fifty thousand and I no get off-days. It is only me guiding dis estate.'

'So, go find a better job! How can you feed over twenty people with that salary?' I responded as we shared a plate of groundnut and hibiscus tea.

'Where? No good job anywhere. My last job was thirty thousand per month. Aunty, Nigeria is hard. Men *dey suffer.*'

I knew he was playing the pity game and hoping the naïve new tenant would be his financial maga, but I didn't mind. He felt like a kindred spirit from the start, so I would always tip him, buy provisions for his children, and even share meals I had cooked with him. And my instinct about him was right; rather than entitlement, he has repaid my every kindness with a small act of goodness of his own. I have never gone out with a dirty car or had to carry anything heavy into my house unassisted in eight months.

'Aunty Ara, you can't park here. Please, ma, I *no fit* lose my job,' Solomon repeats, bringing me back to the present.

I smile at him. 'Solomon, I know. I am not staying. I just want to ask you something.' He leans against my car, smiling back, revealing a row of mostly black teeth.

'Okay, Aunty Ara. How can I *epp* you?'

I push my head out through the window, so I'm close enough to whisper. 'You know that tenant *wey* kill her sugar daddy.' He pretends to think, and I allow him to play ignorant. After a few seconds, his eyes grow two sizes bigger. 'Oh! You mean that Aunty? No o. I don't know her too well, ma. I don't even think I run errands for her.'

'Really?'

He keeps his eyes on the unattended gate. 'Yes, ma. Even that day *wey dey* talk say she kill person. That night I was not around. I *commot*. I get off the next day.'

'Oh.'

His eyes shift back to me, 'Yes. Please, Aunty Ara, you can't park here.'

'Okay, Solomon. Thank you.' I reverse and drive into my allotted parking spot.

Solomon said he never got days off. Which makes sense since he practically lives in the security house.

Strange.

TEN

Hello, Juicy

WEDNESDAY

7.30 a.m.

The traffic on third mainland bridge is notoriously heavy today, so before I head out, I look up alternative routes on the map. Heading downstairs, I smooth out the creases in my mum jeans, which I've paired with a V-neck shirt and sneakers, before stepping out. Solomon acknowledges my wave half-heartedly, avoiding eye contact. I make a mental note to get him a loaf of bread and a big bottle of Coke, maybe even slip him some money for the coming weekend.

When I get to Mafoluku, the parking area is filled with all manner of vehicles, so I drive over to the woman who sells gin in the same compound, opposite the station building. I see her scowling at me as I park in the tight space between two trucks. Getting out of the car, the sun shows no mercy, so I dig my shades out of my bag to protect my eyes.

I walk to the gin seller.

'Good morning, ma. Can I park here?' She smiles at the greeting, a gold front tooth glistening in the sun.

'Good morning, *Sisi*. This Wednesday will favour us all. In Jesus's name, Amen! You can go. Nothing will happen to your car. In Jesus's name, Amen!'

'*Ese* ma. Thank you.'

Walking quickly to get out of the sun's heat, I soon reach the station. The sharp, fishy odour hits my nose as I walk in, and I wince, briefly closing my eyes. I collide with something fleshy and hard, and a low growl prompts me to open my eyes.

'Are you blind? Didn't you see me?' The brawny man before me glares, awaiting an apology.

'Sorry,' I mutter.

He doesn't even respond as he walks away. The fishy stench gets worse with the rising heat in the tiny room. I push through a crowd of people to get to the counter where a stout man in a rumpled uniform screams at the crowd.

'*Sharrap*! Everybody needs to settle down or I will shoot you all!' They immediately fall quiet. He grins and, lowering his voice, asks, 'Now *wetin* happen? Who jam who?'

A man in a saffron shirt and faded purple trousers steps out of the crowd to lean on the counter. 'Thank you, *sah*. This *okada* men *na* him start the accident. He hit me. I hit someone then that person hit the *mezidiz*. Na this *mezidis* driver bring all of us come station!' He points at another man in a singlet and blue jeans, who stands against the door, wailing.

'*Oga*, why you *dey* cry like woman?' The officer speaks to the man in tears.

The man looks up. 'It is my *oga moto dem jam*. How will I pay? Will this Okada man pay or this *napep*?'

Voices are raised again as I scan behind the counter, looking for the woman who was with the deputy on Monday, or someone less belligerent. On the other side of the room, I see an officer reading the newspaper. Once again, I squeeze through the crowd to get to him.

'Good morning. Please, I am looking for the DPO.' He ignores me and continues to read. 'Good morning, sir,' I repeat. He looks up and smiles, his flat nose expanding even more.

'Yes. How can I help you?'

I smile back. '*Oga* DPO asked me to see him today.' He looks me over and then walks into the inner corridor, from where I hear noises from the cells.

The officer yells down the corridor. 'Keep shut there! If you no steal ten thousand from your boss, you *wee* not be here.'

A voice responds, '*Oga*, the man did not pay me for three months. How I *wan* take feed my family?'

'Ehn. You should have steal two thousand naira. Small money that he will not notice! You steal big money, now you are here making noise. Shut up!'

I shift my attention back to the Benz driver and his debacle. He is now seated on a bench with his head between his hands, and six people are kneeling before him.

'Madam! Follow me,' the officer calls out to me. I follow behind him, making sure to avoid the filthy walls.

As we walk past the cells, I look into them, hoping to see Juicy. One of the prisoners, a young man who looks barely eighteen, gives me the middle finger. I scan the other side of the corridor. No sign of her there either.

We walk past the deputy's office and out through the back of the building. The path is jagged with stones and broken concrete, between which thorny plants have sprouted; the hem of my jeans catches on them.

'Sir, did *Oga* DPO move office?' I ask. He ignores me and keeps walking.

We walk for another minute until we reach a building with a sign that reads 'Waiting Room.'

'Aunty, welcome!' The DPO opens the door as soon as we arrive. His head is slightly shiny, and the dye has begun to fade so his baldness is really starting to show.

'Good morning, sir. I hope I am not too early.'

'It's okay, *Sisi*. The police are here to serve you any time, any day. Efficiency is our motto.'

I keep a smile plastered on as he leads me in, dismissing the other officer with his hand. The room's walls are grey and the floor is covered with a seaweed-coloured carpet.

Dark brown leather chairs surround a round wooden table in the middle.

And there, on a two-seater, dressed in black overalls, a taupe vest, and clean rubber slippers, is the infamous, alleged murderer.

The DPO announces, 'This is Juicy. Juicy, this is . . . ' He looks at me and scratches his head as if my name might pop out from his tattooed scalp. 'Oga Yele's, erm—'

'Ara, sir.'

'Ara!' He laughs and then turns to Juicy. 'Answer her, because you know what your lawyer said.'

Juicy nods and he leaves. I am still standing, thinking of how to start the conversation when she speaks.

'Hello, neighbour. Please, sit.'

I sink into the chair nearest to me.

How did she know who I was?

Juicy continues without looking at me. 'I know who you are, and I also know what you do for a living.'

My phone buzzes in my bag so I fish it out to silence it. As I tap the side-button, I see a WhatsApp message from Rude Victoria on the screen:

> As we wait for the three-day ultimatum given to Mr Nicholas to expire, let us see if we can get the agent arrested for this crime of rent increment, we can't allow—

I drop the phone back into my bag.

Juicy continues, 'My neighbour the writer.' Her voice is so soft and quiet that I lean a little closer to hear her.

'Like you can hear me just fine there,' she says. I quickly retract my movement. 'So, Aunty Ara, the writer! Like how can I help you?'

'How do you know who I am?' My voice sounds strained even to my ears.

'Interestingly, like it was Njoku who outed you. He and his friends were debating your three books one evening at Sailor's Lounge. I was curious and looked you up. Imagine my surprise at seeing that it is my neighbour of eight months who has all those useless men screaming and panting.' She winks at me. 'Who is *Oga* Yele?'

'My erm—'

Her eyes twinkle. 'He is your man friend, *abi*?' Her thick, full eyebrows frame big brown eyes that seem to pierce me as she continues to speak. Her naturally pointed nose is bracketed by high cheekbones, and her heart-shaped lips are two-toned, the upper lip dark brown, the lower lip slightly pink. Her fair skin is unmarked and polished.

This kind of beauty can only bring pain.

Juicy clears her throat, and I lower my gaze. 'No, feel free to stare at me. Like I am used to it.' She giggles. 'Okay, Ara. Now, what do you want? Do you want to use me in your next book? Is that it?'

'I don't know yet. If there is a story here, maybe,' I answer truthfully.

'Why? Are you out of ideas?'

'No. Your story doesn't add up, and writing helps me make sense of unclear situations.'

Her eyes suddenly flash with anger. 'Aunty! What is unclear here? Girl kills her sugar daddy. Girl is arrested. Girl is now the country's most talked-about person for the time being. *End of story. Period!*' She pats her hair before she continues. 'And please don't think you are going to save me or write something that will force a proper investigation into my case. Like in my cell alone, there are three people who have been locked up for nearly two months and they say every night that they are innocent of their crimes. I actually believe them, but this is Nigeria! You are not a freedom fighter, nor are you one of those fake Twitter activists.' She stops to drink from a ceramic cup placed on the centre table, then resumes, a little calmer now. 'Besides, they promised they would get me out of here. Sorry, I mean, I will soon get out of here!'

'Who are *they*?'

She covers her mouth, takes a deep breath and replies, 'Ara, please, there is no story here. Period!' I watch as she removes her feet from the slippers and sets them neatly beside a stool. 'If you don't mind, you are supposed to be here for two hours. Like it would be nice if you stay so I can get some sleep. When I wake up, you can go. Thank you.' She stretches out on the two-seater and dozes off in a few seconds, leaving me speechless.

~

An hour later, she stirs awake. A smile lingers around her lips, but her expression slowly dissolves into unfiltered fear when she opens her eyes to see she is still a prisoner. The quiver at the sides of her lips tug at my heart.

No, Ara! Don't feel sorry for her. Get out of here now! Tell Dotun and Susan that you have no story for them.

'You stayed,' she says, as she sits back up in the chair.

'You looked like you needed the rest.'

'I don't get to sleep much. I have to stay awake through the night in case a cellmate or police officer tries to sleep with me.' She stops to check her outfit is not rumpled. 'Okay. So, since you didn't leave, I guess like I owe you one.'

I pick up my bag from the stool beside me. 'No, you don't. I don't want anything in return.'

She ignores my response. 'I'll tell you my story and the events of that day, if you agree to speak to the others.'

'Others?'

'Yes. There are other women involved in this and they'll have to tell you their side, because I don't know how I got here either.' She looks at me, her eyes filling with tears.

'They promised I would only be here for three days if I kept my mouth shut, but it's been five.'

'They? Like other sugar babies?'

'No. Our neighbours.'

ELEVEN

Deep Breath

WEDNESDAY
12.30 p.m.

My palms keep weeping against the car steering, forcing me to tighten my grip. My tummy is hard with tension. All of Juicy's instructions were delivered in a soft and lazy tone, as if we were discussing the weather.

'When you get home, go to House One at seven p.m. Knock, ask for the madam and when she sees you, say the words, "Juicy says *ashewo*". She will then ask you what you want, and you will answer, "I want to rent a secret". Then you can ask about what happened. Don't go there and just say "*ashewo*". You will be beaten if you don't follow exactly what I am saying.'

'Is this a joke? Am I also to do a dance and walk backwards into the house like a witch?'

She answered with a straight face. 'No. Just what I have told you. Nothing else.'

I chuckled. 'It's okay if you don't want to tell me how you got here. You don't have to insult my intelligence.'

Juicy let out such a shrill, snake-like sound that I raised my hands to ward off her anger. 'I am just saying all of this sounds very strange,' I explained.

She laughed. 'Like which part of what is happening in Nigeria looks normal to you? I am in a cell for a crime I had no part in. Almost every person in the country is involved in some kind of scam. Most of our products are fake, including the bottled water. Tons of people are leaving for Canada, and all our presidents rig the elections even though they are too old to lead. Please, stop with the theatrics. Like, don't kill me with laughter.'

'Sorry.'

She closed her eyes, touched her hair and took a deep breath. 'As I was saying, I don't really know what happened that day either. But I know these women and we have a way of doing things. They are like mentors to me. Just do as I told you. Please, no matter how hard they probe you, do not say you are writing about them. Just tell them you are my friend, trying to help with my case. When you learn what you need, go home and write it down.'

I got up and paced the length of the room to keep from looking at her.

'Why will they tell me anything at all?'

'Because they don't know if I have already leaked their secrets to you or anything that incriminates them. They will tell you because they want to know what you know.'

'This is so weird! How long have you known—'

'Don't ask about how long we have known each other. Like we are all neighbours. Not all of us stay locked up in our houses like you. If you want the story about that day, this is how you will get it. Focus on that, the rest is not your business.'

'Okay,' I said. I walked over to the stool and picked up my bag.

'We are going to help each other. I assume that is the point of this visit – to get a story, right? And you will get one.' Her words continued to flow softly from her lips. 'You are the one who wants to tell the story, so you must do what I want, or you won't get to tell it at all.'

'But I won't have a story to publish if I tell the women that I am *not* writing a book? I'll end up being sued! Also, what do you stand to gain in all of this?'

She laughed. 'The book will be my leverage. If they keep their side of the agreement, you can just change the names and tweak the story slightly, creative licence, right? No one will know it's based on anything but your imagination.' She winked at me. 'If they don't get me out, I will give you my written permission to publish the story as I told it to you, with nothing changed. You never know who might read your book and help me. Books travel, do they not? Yours certainly have!'

I gave a half-smile. 'I guess you're right.'

She clapped her hands. 'So, it's settled. We have a deal. You like get a story either way.'

I had so many questions, but I said, 'Okay.'

On my way out, I stopped to thank the DPO in his office. He was talking with a man who was sweating profusely and biting his nails, clearly in distress. As politely as I could, I said, 'Sorry to disturb your meeting, sir. I am leaving. I just wanted to say thank you.'

'You are welcome, my dear sister.'

I whispered, 'I may be coming back tomorrow.'

He rubbed his palms together and smacked his lips. For a moment, I imagined him and Rude Victoria locking lips.

'This place is your home. You are welcome anytime. Police is everybody's friend. See you at the same hour. She will be in the room in the prison backyard.'

'Okay, sir. Thank you.'

TWELVE

Return

WEDNESDAY

1.45 p.m.

Solomon mumbles a half-hearted greeting, looking at the floor as he flings the gate open.

'Solomon, I bought you some bread and Coke,' I say to him before driving in.

He takes it but keeps his gaze lowered. 'Ahh, madam, you try. Thank you.'

I smile at him, seeking eye contact. 'I hope you are not upset with me over that Juicy matter. I was just looking for gist.'

'No problem, ma. If I get any information, I for tell you, but I was not here that day.'

'But Solomon,' I gently coax. 'You are the only gateman we have now. *Abi* Mr Nicholas too *dey* guard gate?'

He laughs. 'Sometimes when I get a family emergency or

small side hustle, I have one person from my state *wey dey* help me. He is a security officer at the hotel close to the gate. He was the one on my shift that day and himself no know when police show to arrest Juicy.'

No wonder he's been acting strange. He didn't want me to know he was not at his duty post.

I respond, 'No wahala. Solomon, you are my person. Don't worry, I won't tell Mr Nicholas.'

His relief is visible. 'Thank you, ma.'

'*Haba* now, Solomon, you are my guy,' I reassure him.

He salutes me and I watch through my rear-view mirror as he mutters to himself then takes a large swig from the bottle of Coke. A few minutes later, I walk into the house. Did today really happen?

THIRTEEN

Decisions

WEDNESDAY

6.45 p.m.

In the social media age, we are all neighbours.

It's like we are all living side by side, cramped like Titus fish in a rolled-back tin. Like, if I stretch my neck out of my window, the spicy aroma of the fried plantain and palm oil beans that you just posted a photo of on Instagram will waft its way to my nostrils. Never mind that I live in the heart of Ikoyi and you in Magodo. Social media is a creature with innumerable eyes, ears and noses invading everyone's lives.

Recently, I watched a live video of an influencer secretly following another girl to Balógun market to confront her over unpaid debts. Was I shocked? Yes. Did that stop me from watching the whole three-hour mess of catfights, crying, cursing and the accidental glimpse of underwear that just happened to be from the brand linked in the influencer's bio? Absolutely not! I have even set an alert for the part two, which drops in two weeks. The savage side of me enjoys watching the chaos unleashed by social media. It has kept me company for eight months, but I don't ever want to be a part of it. My books bring enough attention my way, but not the kind that makes people pry into my personal life.

But if I do this thing Juicy says, I may just end up on social media. Not because of a book plot; for scandal.

Still.

There is no length I wouldn't go for a story. This I know about myself. My stories are my children. They are all I have. Storytelling is my love. So, if I must bare my soul to my neighbours in order to get what I need for this book, then that is exactly what I will do.

What's the worst that could happen? I become a subject of online gossip? That's a small price to pay. Besides, scandal sells books faster.

I check my phone. It is six-fifty p.m. I guess I am going to House One after all.

CHARACTERS

FOURTEEN

Dear Neighbour

WEDNESDAY
6.59 p.m.

I am standing in front of House One. My heart rate quickens, moving at the pace of an angry cheetah running towards prey, and my clammy palms moisten my floral halter-necked dress. I knock on the door. Waiting. No one answers but I see a bell on the side, so I tap it.

'Yessss . . . ?' A tinny voice responds immediately from the speaker.

'Good evening!'

'Aunty, please step back a bit, you are shouting.'

I take a step back and whisper, 'Sorry, and good evening. I am looking for madam, please. I live in House Five.'

A heartbeat later, I hear someone at the door, complaining. 'This door *na wa*. And this estate manager no *gree* fix *am*!' The person finally wins the tug of war and the door swings open. A woman who looks like she is in her late thirties, with unusually big ears, stands in the doorway. 'Good evening. Is my madam expecting you?'

'Yes, she is.' *Might as well start with the lies I mean to go on with.*

The woman steps aside. 'Please come in and wait for her. Madam *dey* upstairs.'

I follow her down a hallway decorated with alabaster statues of naked figures, until we reach a living room that is twice the size of mine. Everything in the house is white, except for the appliances, which are jet black.

There's no way I am paying the same rent as this woman.

I check my watch – it is five past seven. I hear rushed footsteps on the stairs, and my heart starts to pound again.

The mistress of the house appears with the maid. She's dressed in a white jumpsuit, her hair pulled back into a ponytail that looks too tight. There is something familiar about her, but I don't want to stare so I dismiss the thought.

'Good evening. Ola tells me I was expecting you. Do we know each other?'

'Good evening,' I respond.

'How can I help you?'

You can help me by telling me what I am doing here.

'Juicy says *ashewo*.' *There.* I say it. The maid looks confused. Her mistress's face hardens.

'Ola, go outside,' she says.

The maid turns to her. 'Ma?'

'Go out! Now!' The maid leaves. 'What do you want?' she asks as soon as we are alone.

'I want to rent a secret.'

'Why?'

'Because Juicy wants to know what happened before she got here that night.'

'Who the hell are you?'

'I am your neighbour, and I am sent by Juicy.'

She chuckles. 'I figured that much! I mean, why are you here, asking questions?'

'Like I said, I just need to find out about—'

'—the day Njoku died.'

After what seems like an eternity, she continues, 'Take all of your clothes off. To rent a secret, you must first be naked, and then you can get dressed again before we exchange truths.' She eyes me warily. 'Did she not tell you?'

Whoa. She certainly did not!

I stand up from the sofa and quietly slip out of my dress and underwear, feeling awkward. Her jumpsuit falls onto the white tiles.

'If it's okay with you, I would like to keep this on.' She taps her bra and briefs. 'I am not comfortable being naked in front of other women.'

I want to point out the irony of telling me this after

I have already stripped myself down, but I simply say, 'Okay.'

We look at each other, our eyes travelling at the same time from head to toe.

'Are you done?'

'Huh?'

'Are you done looking?' She walks over to a chair and stands before it, facing me. 'That girl has not been in police custody for more than a week, and she wants to come out? This generation and their lack of tolerance for pain. Fucking Gen Z!' She laughs and then sits. I make to sit too. 'Fuck, no! You are not sitting naked on my furniture. Please, go to the backyard and wait for me there. It's straight down the corridor and through the back door.'

I put my dress back on and follow her directions. I open the door to the backyard to find a lounge chair. I stand by it and wait. She comes out, fully dressed now.

'Sit,' she says.

'So, this thing is true?' I ask as she sinks down beside me, her arm grazing mine slightly.

'Yes, it is.' She side-eyes me. 'Please, tell me your secret and let's be quick!'

Ahhh. This one is Juicy's elder sister in rudeness.

I look straight ahead as I say, 'My name is not Ara Ikoyi. It's Bawarin Bello.'

She tilts her head. 'How is that a secret, madam? Wait

a minute – I know that name. Ara . . . wait, are you the writer?!'

Shit. This woman reads.

'Yes.'

'Fuck me! I know you!' She turns to face me and looks me dead in the eye. 'Are you writing a story?'

'The deal is a secret for a secret.'

She moves even closer and whispers into my left ear, 'I was born with both male and female organs.'

I feel the ground shift.

What!!!

'Please, if you are feeling dizzy, move to the floor. That way if you vomit, it won't stain my furniture.'

I glance at her lower body. I can't help myself. And there it is. A slight bulge.

She crosses her legs. 'Let's move on to Juicy's secret. I gave her my car to escape in, the day Njoku died. I figured if she took a vehicle other than her own, she wouldn't be stopped. I still don't know how she managed to land herself in police custody.' She stands up. 'Look here, Bawarin. I must not appear in your story! It won't end well for you.'

I look up at her. 'I am not writing a story. I just want to help Juicy.'

'I have said my own.' She disappears back into the house.

As I leave through the front door, my elbow brushes against Ola, who is waiting to see me out, her eyes shooting daggers at me. No doubt because I called her madam an *ashewo.* I walk quickly back to my house, shut the door, and sink to the floor.

What in the name of witchcraft is going on in this estate?!

FIFTEEN

Past Life

WEDNESDAY
10.50 p.m.

Bawarin clawed her way from Ogbomosho to Lagos on a bus. Bawarin is a sad story. I can no longer bear such sorrow. There are only so many tears my eyes can shed.

Being Ara Ikoyi is a much better deal for me.

Ara is from a middle-class family, an only child who likes to keep her family out of the public eye. Ara's Instagram is mainly focused on her writing, but it suggests she can also have fun. Sometimes, she posts cute pictures that are sexy enough to make men drool, but most of the time she's in work mode. Ara is a bestselling author who may not be well known among her neighbours, but is widely read internationally. Ara is everything Bawarin dreamt of being and more.

I step away from the steamed-up bathroom mirror, unwilling to look at my face.

SIXTEEN

A Day for Gluttons

THURSDAY

8.50 a.m.

Driving down to the station, I wonder if I am a glutton for punishment, but this coven business on the estate is the most exciting thing to happen to me this year. Last night, I dreamt of flying brooms, faded wrappers and women whose breasts unified as one, with legs that became guns shooting at nothing. My writing brain cells are in hyperdrive.

Besides, I want to take some food to Juicy, if she will accept it. She needs to eat to keep up her strength. Before I leave, I grab a breath freshener from my kitchen cabinet so that when she is done eating, the officers won't smell it on her.

As I left the house, I caught a glimpse of myself reflected in the vase in my hallway. The overpriced, coral, Mai Atafo blouse I have on complements my caramel skin tone, along with thick black leggings which accentuate my curves. A wristwatch, pearl earrings and blue sneakers complete the look. Thankfully, I managed to pull my hair into a low ponytail with the ends woven into a single weave.

Not bad for someone who didn't get much sleep.

The traffic today is heavy. A long trailer fell on an SUV, crushing it instantly. Both sides of the road are blocked with cars and onlookers who are either wailing or recording the gory scene on their phones. I wonder if the casualties have people who will remember them. Last month, *Ristablog* put up a post about a man who had lain dead in a morgue in Ebonyi State for more than thirty days, and no one had come to claim his body.

A hundred metres from the scene, I see the half-naked man who attacked my taxi on Monday, chasing a woman with an umbrella.

This is the last time I will take this route. I refuse to run into this man again!

Ten minutes later, the traffic starts to move. As I approach the station, my phone rings.

'Yessss, Dotun? Why are you calling me?'

'Ara, your book has been longlisted for the Women's Prize for Fiction in the UK! We just received the news. This is *huge.* The announcement will be made next month, so please keep it to yourself for now.'

'Which book?!'

'The third one, of course – that's the only one eligible for entry because it was published in the last year.'

'Oh, my days! That's wonderful! Congratulations to all of us! Team work makes the dream work.'

I'm in the compound, trying to find a place to park as we speak. I drive into a spot so close to the wall of the station that I barely have space to open my door to get out. Dotun's voice draws me back. 'I am so proud of you, Ara. Keep writing, okay?'

Before stepping out of the car, I take a moment to read up on the Women's Prize for Fiction nominees for the previous year. The list is impressive. I am familiar with most of the other authors' works. If the fellow nominees for this year are just as good, I will be lucky to get shortlisted. But with the longlist alone, Susan can negotiate better deals for me.

My phone buzzes. *Speak of the devil.* It's an email from Susan. Are these women joined at the hip? I walk towards the entrance of the police station.

Here we go again.

~

The police station is not as packed as it was yesterday, but there are a handful of people hawking bread, their trays covering the counter. While no one is looking, one of the officers helps himself to two loaves. The chaos masks his theft. A broad-shouldered woman speaks to another officer who is struggling to write with his notepad balanced on top of the bread.

'If dem no let us sell bread for that site, how will we make money? The site workers buy all of our bread in three hours, which is very good for business. Now, the *omo onile* say we must dash them two dozen loaves every morning. *Oga* police, me that I am selling the bread, I have not eaten up to twelve loaves in one month before in my life. I don't even eat bread, I drink garri! How will I now give two dozen to another human being! That is my profit *omo onile* wants to chop.'

'So, what do you want us to do for you?' the officer writing stops to ask.

'They should let us sell our bread as usual. We are not giving them anything for free.'

'Madam, that one will be hard o. If you want to solve this matter, give them three loaves, and send two to the station every morning,' he says with a wink.

Another vendor, standing behind the first woman, says, 'Later on, you police officers will say the police are here to serve you! You are the one asking for a bribe!'

The officer responds, 'So, police no go chop? How will we fight *omo onile* if our bellies are empty? That one is not bribe. You are helping us so we can help you.'

'Madam, follow me!' The officer I met on the second day calls out to me. 'You are the one from *Oga* Yele?'

Ah yes, Yele, I really should respond to his calls and messages. He could shut down this entire thing with Juicy if he senses I am avoiding him. That man is petty.

'Yes,' I respond.

'Madam, do quick! Come with me!' the officer repeats, this time pointing his baton at me. *It's like this one is not okay. Didn't his boss give him part of the two hundred dollars?*

I follow him with more confidence this time, since I know where we are headed. When we arrive at the door, Juicy is the one who greets us.

'Thank you, Daddy.' She kneels.

He touches her shoulders. 'You are welcome. Two hours, okay? Hurry, you have to clean the latrine today and the girls are waiting to see if you will do *ojoro*.' She laughs and he joins in. I see from her eyes that she is angry, but this man doesn't know it. He leaves.

'Did you go to our neighbour?' she asks before I've even sat down. I don't respond. I take out the food I've brought with me and lay it on the table.

'They told me on the first day that you had not eaten. I brought this just in case,' I say as I lay out the cutlery.

She looks at me and starts to laugh in an ugly way. She barks, 'You really think food is my biggest problem? Didn't you hear that man say I have to wash pit latrine after our session?'

Aunty, if you didn't want to wash anything, you should not have killed your sugar daddy, I think. Out loud, all I say is, 'I am sorry.'

'Besides, you can't curry favour with me so easily. Did you do as I instructed?' she asks while tearing open the paper bag to get to the food inside.

'I did. Is it okay to ask a few questions?'

She arches an eyebrow. 'Sooo polite. Yes, ask.'

'What is with the process of getting naked to rent a secret? Why all the ritual?'

'Life is a ritual, Aunty Ara.'

'Why did you not mention it yesterday?'

She shrugs. 'You were expressing shock instead of paying close attention to my instructions. So, I decided to let you find out on your own. Besides, do you have a problem with nudity?'

I hope the food chokes her a little.

She stops chewing to drink some water.

Good. Maybe the pepper will shut you up.

I say to her, 'It's just so—'

'Is the secret you are telling not already making you naked?' she says as she bites into the goat meat. 'The point of taking your clothes off is that people will do anything to sell a story these days. This sickening urge to record everything consumes us all. So, going naked is an assurance for you and the other women. All you have as witnesses are your ears.' She takes another bite, chews for a while, then speaks.

'The secrets you exchange are for insurance purposes. If you snitch on them, they will also sell you out, Madam Writer.'

I swallow my many questions except the most important one. 'So, what's next?'

She coughs. 'Let me finish eating, it's like you put extra pepper in this food to punish me. In the meantime, you can get ready to record.'

I place my phone down on the table.

SEVENTEEN

Juicy's Confession I

THURSDAY
10.18 a.m.

Um, I know people look at me and think, *Juicy is just a sugar baby. She is one of those girls that don't like to work. They just want to lie down and let men fuck them, then pay for their lifestyle.*

Let's look at this logically. Like, let's engage our brains!

Is it lying down that got me this life? Is my vagina that special? No! What got me here is my hustler spirit. I gave my beauty and my vagina to the highest bidder because I have other people relying on me for their survival. I literally could not afford to cheapen my vagina. Not in a country like Naija. Do you know how many beautiful girls fuck for free under the bridge in Ojuelegba? Do you know how many beautiful girls are married to sorry excuses for men? If you see the fine girls I grew up with, and where they've ended up, you will know that beauty is not enough.

First, I had to do a lot of research to find where the rich men were. I invested in clothes, my looks, and everything. Then I worked on my speech and carriage. Do you think if I looked like a pepper seller and screamed like a conductor, Njoku would have talked to me? Finding a rich sugar daddy is like finding a great job in Nigeria. You must be well-connected and informed. Neither brains nor beauty means anything if you don't know the right people in this country.

I actually quit being a sugar baby twice. I would tell myself to quit and then chicken out. However, I was able to follow through with my decision on two occasions. I'll tell you about the second one first.

The second time I decided I was going to stop, I applied for over twenty paid internships. I was invited to fourteen interviews. Every single one of them was a joke. One of the offices I went to looked like a voodoo priest's shrine. It was a miracle that I was able to get away from there without losing any body parts. Another office had a manager who farted throughout the interview, and none of the other panellists could call him out. I recall that after one of the interviews, a female HR manager advised that I focus on finding a husband, not a job, before I finished my studies. Still, I didn't let any of this break my spirit. I kept going for the interviews.

It was the final screening that showed me once and for all that I was wasting my time trying to live a 'respectable' life. Once the interview was done, the HR man slipped his number into my file and told me to come to his hotel for the second part of the hiring process. As if I would have screwed that frog-like creature, and all for seventy thousand naira a month. My sister, at that point, I threw myself back into being a sugar baby.

Now the day Njoku died, the car I had borrowed from the neighbour you saw last night, broke down in Ikeja. I was on my way to Badagry to stay with my aunty. The other women had advised that I go somewhere else until the police found whoever had killed Njoku, rather than staying in the house where he had died. When the car broke down, I took it as a sign to go back and collect some important things I had forgotten. I called one of the women on the estate, who told me I could come back to get them. I returned to the house to pick up my laptop for university and the ATM card Njoku had given me.

I calculated that by the time I returned, the car would be fixed, and I could go on. I booked an Uber to take me home and found the police waiting for me. I walked right into their trap. Somehow, the police found out about Njoku's death and arrived within two hours! This is Nigeria. No one is more incompetent than the police. So, whatever she told you about wanting to help me is a lie. Why did the neighbour's car break down? I am not saying *she* necessarily set me up, but *someone* did, and the whole point of you exchanging secrets with them is to help me find out who landed me in here!

Anyway, back to that day. The police brought me here to Mafoluku, and they put me in a cell and told me what to write in my statement. An hour later, Njoku's wife showed up with lots of cameras and reporters. They threw questions, insults and words at me. She kept weeping and hitting me.

Like the funny thing is, she knows her husband is a popular community penis, so I don't understand why she was crying and cursing me that day. I don't understand all the drama she comes to display here.

It's fine *sha*, please I need you to go to House Nine this evening at eight p.m. Repeat the same process and then whatever she tells you, please make sure to act on it. Thank you for the meal. Maybe bring something with less spice next time.

Now, I need to sleep. You heard the buffoon. I have to clean that disgusting place after you leave.

EIGHTEEN

Crazy Things

THURSDAY
12.10 p.m.

Once Juicy wakes up, I head out. I stop to say a quick goodbye to the DPO, with the promise of returning the next day. My phone rings as I get onto Osborne Road.

'Hi, Yele.'

'*Ahn ahn*, Madam Writer, so after using me to get access to Juicy, you can't be bothered to pick up my calls?'

'I am sorry, I have been—'

'Busy? I know. You know what, baby? Let's grab dinner tonight. My trip was shorter than I expected. So, I am back in town.'

'I can't. I have a few things to do.'

He sighs. 'What are you busy with, Ara? You are not on a book tour. Didn't you just finish one in December?'

'I have a date.'

He laughs. 'A date that I am sure will end badly. You will be back. This is what we do. You know I am in love with you, Ara.' He starts to sing, 'Baby *mi jowo, je ka jo ma gbadun.*'

'Yele, Yele, please let's talk another time. I don't want to get stopped by the road safety officials.'

'Where?! They can't touch you—'

'Let's talk later.'

I end the call and turn into the street that leads to the estate. Once I am close, I park, wondering if I even want to go in. Nine months ago, I remember thinking if I managed to get a house in this estate, I would have sealed my status as part of the urban elite. I would truly become an *ará Ikoyi*. Now, I am not so sure.

What kind of housing agent only rents houses to women? I have tried to reach Mr Nicholas for information on Juicy, but his number has been unavailable. According to Rude Victoria's last WhatsApp message, his phone has been switched off since he made the announcement about increasing the rent. I don't blame him, though. I understand running from your demons all too well.

The only problem is they eventually catch up with you.

~

I sit in the tub and watch as it slowly fills. I have a few hours before my next meeting. Should I write? Maybe I should issue a response to the emails from my publishers here in

Africa about doing readings in Mauritius and Kigali to soft launch my fourth book.

Nope.

I watch as the bubbles dance around the tub. How did a man die in this estate, and no one heard anything? How are all these women related to Juicy, and what is the main secret they are hiding? And where was I when all of this happened? Sure, I was busy wallowing in my writerly misery, but I went out when necessary, so how did I miss all the drama? The day Juicy reportedly killed Njoku, I recall Solomon came to my flat.

'Aunty, do you want some palm wine?'

'Solomon, are you now a palm wine tapper?'

'One of my wife bring some from the village so I want to give to my favourite tenants.'

I laughed and accepted his offer. The palm wine was delicious. I slept like a baby.

The phone rings from where I've left it on a stool near the tub, shaking me out of my thoughts. I sink deeper into the tub, briefly submerging myself.

~

After my bath, I go downstairs to get some food. I need all the strength I can muster before I have to remove my clothes in front of another stranger. As the *efo riro* heats up in the microwave, I walk through to the dining area which doubles as my writing space. I see a thin layer of dust on the vintage typewriter that I purchased in an auction and the notepad where I used to scribble my ideas. I take a dish towel from the kitchen and start to wipe the area clean. The microwave beeps but I am no longer hungry.

I dust, wipe, spray till everywhere shines. I run upstairs to fetch my phone. I play Juicy's confession from the start, then start to jot on my notepad with a pencil. I describe Juicy as I know her and then recreate a fictional version of her. I do this with everyone I have spoken to so far. After an hour, I open my laptop to type, beginning with my author's note.

Dearest Gentle Readers,

The weight of success can give you a hunchback. Before I became a writer, I used to wonder how it was that some authors, after one successful book, never wrote again. *Why would this person stop at one book?* I would groan in frustration, wanting more.

Now that I am an author who sometimes has thoughts of drinking poison, I understand why.

My dear readers, the source of my hunchback, this book is personal to me, I am not writing this just for the sake of making another bestseller list. This is not some imaginary story. It is about my neighbour who allegedly killed her sugar daddy. I hope you can step into her shoes as you read.

I can't promise another story any time soon. But please, enjoy this one.

All my love,

Ara Ikoyi

I am certain Susan won't let me keep this note in the manuscript that she submits to publishers, but it is fun to include, just to read her response. I start writing chapter one, introducing Juicy's world.

After a while, the alarm on my phone goes off.

It's time to go to House Nine.

~

Standing at the entrance of House Nine wearing an *adire buba* and a blue denim skirt that dances above my knees, I check my reflection in the window beside the door. The fluorescent yellow light above me helps me see as I readjust my skirt. My watch buzzes. It's a minute to nine. I knock.

The door opens but there is no one in sight.

'Who are you?'

The voice startles me. I look down to see a little boy with black curly hair, wearing only a pair of pants. He puts out his hand and drags me into the house.

'I am looking for your mummy,' I say, hoping that I'm actually talking to my neighbour's son.

He turns his face towards the staircase, calling: 'Mummy, you have a visitor!'

A coarse voice screams back, 'Daniel, I have told you to use the intercom. Don't shout like a village boy. Where is Philo?'

'Aunty Philo went to buy water!'

'And she left you alone? Honestly, that girl is useless. I am coming, dear.'

I hear footsteps. Two minutes later, the hulking woman who was at the tenants' meeting appears. *Oh, this was the boy she had with her that day.* There is something familiar about her face, though I'm not sure what it is. I try to think, but my pounding heart makes it hard to concentrate. *Stop worrying about what these women look like, Bawa. That is not why you are here.*

She approaches me. 'How did you get in?'

I point to her son. 'He let me in.'

'Daniel. How many times must I tell you—'

'Sorry, Mummy.'

'Go to your room before I spank you!'

The boy climbs the stairs, stopping halfway to look at me and stick out his tongue, before vanishing up the stairs.

The woman walks behind me to shut the front door firmly. My pulse slows, so I look around to avoid staring at her thick legs, which are on display beneath her knee-length orange dress. The walls are painted teal, and most of the furniture is upholstered in dark red leather. The house seems smaller than the one I visited yesterday. It's closer in size to mine, but the chandeliers hanging from the ceiling make it look more like a showroom. The woman's voice interrupts my inspection.

'I know you. You are the writer we visited—'

'Juicy says *ashewo*,' I say. *I don't have time for chitchat.*

'Don't be rude, dear. At least let me finish my sentence.' She looks at me, kisses her teeth and says, 'What do you want?'

'I want to rent a secret for Juicy.'

'Why?'

'She wants to know what happened before she got here that day.'

She unzips her dress and pulls it down to her waist, revealing an orange lace bra. She starts to push the dress down to her knees. She stops midway to look at me. 'Are you here to watch a strip show?' She steps out of the dress to reveal matching orange knickers. There are long stripes of mottled skin, running from her bosom to her navel, and she smiles as if to say, *I dare you to ask me what happened.*

I take my clothes off too.

She peels her brassiere off, and the knickers.

'Okay, now that we can both see we are not hiding any microphones or cameras, shall we?' she says once my eyes travel back to hers. We dress again in silence, the air filled with the tension of unspoken words.

She points to the door leading out of the living room. 'Please go to the backyard.'

'Alright.' My voice comes out as a timid squeak. I find the backyard easily, and there, placed against the back wall of the house, is a teal-coloured two-seater. I stare at it, but I do not sit.

'You first!' Her voice startles me and my heart starts to pound again. I turn around and she is standing so close to me that I can see the hairs in her nostrils. I whisper in her ear; the scent of lavender barely masking sweat hits me.

'I suffer from impostor syndrome. I don't know how I got to this level of success as a writer.'

She leans back and for a second, I think she doesn't buy my secret. But she says, alarmed, 'Are you going to write about Juicy? Is that what this is about?'

'No, I am just helping her.'

Looking relieved, she pulls me in and speaks into my ear. 'I am a businesswoman. I steal artefacts from museums and sell them to private collectors abroad. Of course, I have agents who do the actual stealing for me. Business has been slow since the pandemic, but this is my main job.' She rubs her left thigh and continues, 'Also, I was married, but my husband left me because I could not give him children.'

I clasp my hands together. 'I am sor—'

She laughs. 'Don't worry, I took his legs. I pushed him down the staircase one night when he came home drunk, reeking of another woman's scent.' She touches my left shoulder. 'You don't leave a woman for something she has no control over. No one prays to be infertile. Marriage is for better or for worse.' She scratches her right ear, making a *tsk*-ing sound with her mouth. 'To comfort myself after his paralysis, I adopted a boy from my village, that naughty boy who opened the door for you. That's him. So, my dear, it is just me, my son and the maid! We are enjoying Lagos. My husband is in a home for disabled, somewhere in the east.' She moves over to the two-seater and sits down. 'Now Juicy has brought us all this unnecessary attention with this murder case.'

I take a seat next to her, waiting. I feel like I just got a bargain, three secrets for the price of one.

She continues, 'So, to Juicy's secret. I was the one who found Njoku dead. Juicy was not at home. Oh, by the way, I have the forms for her university graduation. Maybe you can help her submit them, so she can still graduate.'

Graduate? From a cell? Wait, what did she just say?

'How did you find him dead in someone else's flat?'

She laughs. 'That's because I have keys to everyone's apartment in the estate.'

My eyes widen. 'That's not right!'

'*That is not right!*' She mimics me, then crosses her legs. 'I keep them in case of emergencies. I can enter your apartment to save myself and you. I don't have yours though because you keep changing your locks.' She gets up. 'I think that's enough secrets for one day.'

A chill descends in the night air. 'I'll take the papers,' I say.

We go back inside, and she goes upstairs to fetch them while I wait by the front door. She comes back and hands them to me. 'Here you go.'

'Thank you.' I turn the doorknob, but her voice stops me.

'Juicy will be fine. Life makes us strong when it slaps us the hardest.'

I look at her, confused. 'What if she doesn't get out?'

'She will. She is a smart girl. She will figure it out.'

Am I hearing right? They all keep saying the same thing about Juicy, so why did they act like they didn't know her five days ago?!

NINETEEN

Write or Wrong

THURSDAY

11.25 p.m.

According to *whoever* made the rules, a writer should look and sound a specific way. I don't have that look or sound. I don't have an MFA in creative writing from a prestigious institution abroad. What I have is trauma that success has shrouded. It still simmers under it all. My art derives from it and I suspect that it will be the source for a long time.

When I left Ogbomosho, I came to Lagos with a nylon bag full of clothes, eleven thousand naira, a notebook containing all my writing, and a flash drive with the email addresses of all the publishers in Nigeria that I had compiled over the years.

My plan was to sleep under a bridge until I made enough money from menial jobs to start paying rent somewhere. Once I had a roof over my head and better clothes, I would go around to family houses, offering my services as a tutor to their children, and spend any free time typing up my novels in an internet café so that I could send them out to publishers. Eventually, I would become a successful writer. No matter how long it took.

Lady Luck was kind to me, and I met a man called Godsword on the bus from Ogbomosho to Lagos. As he sat beside me, I noticed his sculpted jawline and huge hands. He was built like a bouncer. We started to chat, and he revealed that he had visited Ogbomosho for an old school friend's wedding. His late father had owned a fleet of one-bedroom apartments in Agege, which he had willed to him as his share of the inheritance, and Godsword had now been a landlord for six months. I told him my father had thrown me out of the house because I had slapped his second wife.

'Don't worry, I will help you. We who have no parents must help one another. Do you have somewhere to stay?'

'No, I don't. I—'

'You can stay with me until you find a place. Lagos is not for the faint-hearted. And you are a fine girl,' he said, after I told him it was my first time in the city. He squeezed my hand and bought me walnuts, *akara* and bread to keep me going on our journey. He kept smiling at me and offering to buy more things. I was not stupid, I knew if I wanted to stay with him without paying rent, I had to give up something.

That night, in his room – one of the studio apartments his father had left him – as the candle burned slowly in the corner, I fucked him. I made sure he used a condom, of course.

One week became one month, and before I knew it, a year had passed. We found a rhythm: I cooked, cleaned, kept my legs open and in return, he gave me a roof over my head. Most evenings, after we had eaten, as we sat out on his balcony, he would say, 'Bawa, we could leave this place and use the money I earn from my rentals to get somewhere nice in Alagbado. We could even get married *sef.*'

'No problem,' I would respond.

During my stay with him, I started tutoring his tenants' children. I was making five hundred naira per student every week.

There were three types of tenants in Godsword's building. First, the ones whose children I was tasked with teaching. One of the students, a boy called Moruf, had devised an alternative alphabet song, which he would recite: 'A for Anger, B for Beating . . . ' He screamed whenever I asked him to recite the proper version.

'Moruf, it is A for Apple, B for Ball.'

'Aunty teacher Bawa, I no *sabi* apple. It is what they are teaching me in school, I am saying to you.' No matter how hard I tried, Moruf would not learn.

The second type of tenants were those who knew I was

Godsword's girlfriend, and they made snide remarks to me daily, like:

'If me too I fine like you, I will not pay rent now. I will use my bottom power.'

'Godsword toasted my sister o, it is me that I didn't let her date him. See now, we for *don dey* live for free inside Agege.'

Then there were the tenants who believed that if they were kind to me, they would not have to pay the monthly rent.

'Fine Bawa, please take this fish. Cook for the landlord, you hear?'

'Thank you.'

'No, don't thank me. In fact, I will bring you some oranges tomorrow.'

'Okay, thank you.'

At the end of the month, once Godsword stepped out to go to work, the tenants would appear at our door. 'Bawa, Bawa, my rent is not complete o. How will we do it? *Ehn ehn*, I hope you enjoyed the fish? Please help us talk to your boyfriend, *abi* are you people married?'

That period in Agege, now that I reflect on it, was a good time. Godsword's job in the rubber manufacturing factory, along with the rent from the properties, kept us comfortable. Three months into the relationship, he bought me a phone.

'I am in love with you. Once we have made enough money, we will marry. Don't worry, Bawa. I will look after you.'

But I knew I wanted more, and when I was not teaching, cooking or cleaning, I kept submitting my manuscript and working on making it better, using the computer centre opposite the house.

The tepid responses from publishers fuelled me. One wrote: *This book is too weird.* Another said: *Your language is not poetic enough. It's a little pedestrian.* But I didn't give up.

Finally, a small publisher called Pata Pata Press responded to a query with: *Your book has potential. We will be in touch.* The owners of the publishing house were called Khibi and Kema, two brothers who ran the business together. I remember doing a small dance of victory and even as I taught the students that week, I kept smiling. I knew my dream of becoming a writer was getting closer to reality. So, I pestered Pata Pata Press till they agreed to see me.

That day, I took some money and boarded a bus to the coffee shop on the border between Obalende and Ikoyi where we had arranged to meet.

'Your manuscript is fine. But the Nigerian literary scene needs great writing if you want to see your book sell,' Khibi said to me as he sipped his coffee, his glasses sitting halfway down his nose bridge. He wore a plain white T-shirt, black trousers and black palm slippers. His brother sat beside him in a matching outfit – except without the glasses.

'I am willing to work on any notes you send to me, sirs.'

Khibi asked, 'Are you sure you don't want anything to eat or drink?'

'No, sir, I am fine, thank you,' I responded, hoping the growl in my tummy didn't betray me as the smell of oatmeal cookies wafted past my nose.

'Okay. One more thing, my brother and I think that your name, Bawarin Arabambi, is not marketable because people might find it difficult to pronounce. If you can find a better pen name and make the manuscript shine, I can offer you a contract.'

'I can do all of that, sir.'

'Don't call me sir. Call me Khibi. So, tell us a bit about you.'

'My name, as you know, is Bawarin, and the only thing I want to be is a writer. Right now, I work as a tutor.'

'Oh, good. You need a side hustle because writing alone can't sustain you.'

I nodded. 'Okay, sir. Is it okay to ask what you do apart from publishing?'

'I am a writer. Although I am too busy to write nowadays. My brother is my partner. Silent partner in the business and in everything, it would seem.' He laughed at his last line.

'That's all you do?'

'Yes.'

'And you both came in that car?' I pointed to the grey Range Rover parked outside.

He looked at me wearily. 'Your point?'

I smiled at them. 'Writing will sustain me too. My books will earn me money.'

Kema chuckled and finally spoke. 'Hmmm. For a girl that has written a half-baked manuscript with a pen name that doesn't sparkle, you are quite confident.'

'I have faith in myself.'

Khibi played with the rim of the cup. 'You left your manuscript untitled, with a note saying, *To be revealed in person*. It was one of the things that caught our eye, aside from your catchy first line.'

'Yes, I wanted to talk to you about the title in person, in case I needed to convince you.'

He dropped his hands to the table and leaned forward. 'Okay? What is the title?'

'*How to Murder your Parents*.'

He looked at me. His eyes grew bigger as if I had just offered him a delicious meal after years of starvation. 'I love the title! Yes, now I want to know more.' He threw his head back and laughed.

Kema kept watching me, the steam from his tea giving him a mysterious aura as he sat back. The meeting wrapped, with Khibi promising to be in touch.

After they left, I stayed behind at the coffee shop because I wanted to see how the other half lived before I went back to Agege. I also needed to think of a pen name that could work for readers. As people came in, I eavesdropped on their conversations and watched as they interacted with one another. The women wore *boubous* or T-shirts and jeans, their hair was not tucked under wigs as I had expected and every one of them wore the shade of skin they were born with proudly. The perfumes the men wore announced their presence before their entry, and most of them moved at a pace that would make the people who lived on the mainland throw curses at them. Everything was well-paced, yet timely. I learnt an important lesson that day – there are levels to wealth. These people in Ikoyi were wealthy, not rich. They didn't need to scream their wealth, it moved silently with them.

I realised that I wanted to be someone who could live in Ikoyi and move the way all these women with their natural hair did. I basked in the luxury of their various accents, which I imagined had been influenced by their travels. I wanted to be part of their world, so I made the decision then and there to change my name to Ara Ikoyi, meaning part of the Ikoyi circle. I cut off my permed hair at the local barber's shop in my area that evening, so it could grow naturally.

'So, you are going to look like a man now, Bawa,' Godsword whined as he watched the barber scrape everything off my head.

'It will grow back, my love.'

'This your forehead is too big, you need hair to cover

it. I pity you, the sun will show you who is boss with this your scalp.'

'I'll wear a scarf when I go out.'

Little by little, I worked on all the suggestions sent from Pata Pata Press.

Six months later, they offered me a contract, including two hundred thousand naira as an advance. Godsword also gave me five hundred thousand naira to put towards our wedding. Including the tutoring money I had saved, I had eight hundred thousand in total. I started to look for apartments in Lekki. Eventually, I found a tiny flat in Jakande that was within my budget. Once I had paid the deposit and had the keys to my new house, I began to plan my exit. Two weeks later, Godsword travelled to see his mother in Benue state. I packed my bags and wrote him a letter, thanking him and wishing him the best in life. I also apologised for stealing our wedding savings.

I knew he wouldn't find me. I left Bawarin behind in Agege. I moved to the Island as Ara Ikoyi and focused on my writing. I guess when you are already an orphan with little to no backup plan, the only way is up.

How To Murder Your Parents became my first bestselling book. Everything moved quickly after that. Within five years, I had three books published. *How to Murder your Parents* was an unexpected hit, considering it was my debut. Three years later, now a little more known and successful,

I published *Bodies Bodies Bodies,* which became an international bestseller. And a year after that, *Who Is Afraid of Secrets?* came out, became another international bestseller, and is now longlisted for the Women's Prize for Fiction.

TWENTY

Billboards

FRIDAY

8.30 a.m.

As I cross the bridge on my way to Yaba, heading to the University of Lagos, a new billboard planted in the middle of the lagoon screams at me: promising that ordinary people can be homeowners. I often wonder if there is an organisation somewhere looking into the level of market inflation going on with real estate in Nigeria. Property in this country is blood money repackaged. The last time Mr Nicholas came to the estate, he was in a 2021 Mercedes GLA 250. Perhaps he is hoping to upgrade to a Ferrari with the extra rental income. Everyone seems to be squeezing something out of Juicy's situation. Even me, but at least I'm honest about it.

I descend the third mainland bridge at the first exit and take the turn for Adekunle, Yaba. Some police officers at the traffic light are harassing a bus driver. I accelerate past them before they can stop me. I don't need police *wahala* today. My assignment is to submit Juicy's documents to her department and then get her file signed.

Once on campus, I locate the Department of Mass Communication more easily. The space I parked in the first time is occupied, and I see the guard approaching me. Quickly, I fish out some money from the glove compartment.

'Daddy, good afternoon,' I say before he reaches the car. He stops by the door, and I press the money into his hand. His grumpy face lights up.

'I hope you remember me?'

'Of course, you are the aunty with the fine jeep. The guest lecturer. Follow me. I know where you can park.'

Once I've parked, he leads me upstairs, telling me enthusiastically about how Nigeria is headed for another military coup if the leaders keep disappointing the people. I nod absent-mindedly as I look for the office of the departmental secretary. It is the fourth door on the right of the corridor that leads to the classrooms and lecturers' offices.

'Thank you, sir,' I say. He takes the hint and leaves.

I knock.

'Come in, don't break down our door!'

I walk in and see the noodle-cooking lecturer, Dr Udenwa, hovering over the other woman, Mrs Tinubu, as they go through a list. They look up as I say good morning.

'*Nne*, it is you. I have been looking at the *Arise* page. No posts about my anniversary yet. Why is that?' Her tone is sharp.

'Sorry, Doctor, I have been busy.' I delicately let out the 'doctor' word to appease her. '*Arise News* has told me that until I find enough information on Juicy, I am not allowed to work on any other story. If I do, I will be fired.'

'Hmmm.'

'So, I don't want to lose my job because you and your husband have a wedding anniversary, ma. Sorry, Doctor.'

She looks at me to see if I am being sarcastic. I maintain a blank expression but I see the secretary's lips quiver.

'Did you come to interview me?'

'No, Doctor. I came to submit documents on Juicy's behalf.'

She loses interest. 'Please, send me a link when the article is up. I sent you some pictures and a write up. We have an agreement. Don't forget.'

'Okay, Doctor.'

She walks out, leaving the door slightly ajar. I turn to the secretary.

'Are you Juicy's sister? You resemble small,' she asks.

I know she is pulling my legs, but her flattery makes me smile.

'Yes, ma.'

'Ah ha . . . very gentle girl. Is really a *pirry*. I will file the documents. She will graduate. I have been thinking since say this girl no get family or friends that will help her submit. Thank God you are here.' She laughs, revealing the overlapping arrangement of her yellow teeth. 'She used to give me plenty of money. Very brilliant girl. She is supposed to finish with first class *sef*.' She takes the files, stamps them, and gives me a document. 'Greet Juicy for me. I am praying for her.'

~

Once I arrive back at the police station, I am led to the room where we have been meeting. Juicy is on the two-seater, her back turned to me.

'Juicy, the aunty is here. Cheer up. You are not the first this is happening to.' He turns to leave.

'What happened, sir?' I ask him.

He hangs his head. 'She will tell you.'

I take a seat and set the cooler and the document the secretary gave me down on the table. I can hear Juicy crying.

What do I do now? I don't know how to deal with tears.

After a minute, she sits up and turns to look at me. Her left eye is swollen, and she has a busted lip.

'They have started soiling my fine girl,' she says with a smile, tears still running down her face. 'I don't want to talk about it.' She picks up the paper from the table, reads it and then smiles again. 'Thank you. You were able to submit it.'

I fiddle with my bag before speaking. 'I have painkillers

here with me. I sometimes have migraines because of my work.' I bring out a blister pack of Ibuprofen. She doesn't touch them. Instead, she drops the piece of paper and continues to cry.

'Do you know I am being called the sugar daddy killer on TikTok? Njoku's children and their mother did a live video, claiming I ruined their family.' She taps her chest many times. 'Me?! Small girl like me ruined a family!' Now she chuckles, the tears from her eyes mingling with the snot running from her nose. She takes a few squares of serviettes from the food package I've brought her, and wipes her face gingerly. She smooths her hair.

I say the only words that matter. 'I am so sorry.'

'That stupid girl in the next cell just came in, showed me the recording and gave me a beating. She claimed that I reminded her of the woman who snatched her father from her mother. The officers and other cell mates did nothing to stop her for nearly ten minutes. All the other girls fuck the officers so they can keep their phones and buy food from outside, but I won't do that, so they allow madness to happen to me.'

As she picks up the package, she winces.

'I can feed you,' I offer. She squints at me to see if I am joking.

'*Oya*.' She gestures. I move to the sofa, sitting next to her. Before scooping up a spoonful, I smile.

'I didn't put in too much pepper, but it will still hurt you. I am sorry.'

'It's okay.'

I feed her as gently as I can. I stop to give her water in between mouthfuls and clean the blood from her lips. She eats half of the meal and then rests her head on my shoulder.

'I can come back tomorrow,' I say as she lifts her head and then signals for me to pass her the painkillers. She responds after taking the medication. 'It's okay. Let me sleep for thirty minutes, then we can talk.'

I go back to my seat, and I watch her sleep. I fish out my phone and type an email to Susan:

Dear Susan,

I am so sorry I have been incommunicado. I am still writing, but I should be done soon.

Thank you.

I do not say exactly when, because she will hold me to the deadline. I also email Dotun:

Babes,

Please leave me be for three months.

I need to write.

She responds five minutes later.

Good girl! I hope you have reached oyinbo?

I wonder how she is able to be so quick with her responses, despite having two children. Susan responds ten minutes later.

Hi Ara,

We are so relieved to finally hear from you.

Congratulations on your nomination!

Your PR firm says you have a book tour coming up next year?

We are very excited, and looking forward to seeing you, and I am so looking forward to reading your new work.

All best,

Susan

I send a text to my carpenter to come change my locks in the evening.

'Let's start. Are you ready to record?'

Juicy is awake.

TWENTY-ONE

Juicy's Confession II

FRIDAY
11.03 a.m.

Just look at! On everything, I swear I am going to delete that bitch that beat me when I get out of here. She started a fight with me over food. Food I didn't even want. Like look at me! I am bruised in places no one should ever be.

See, I was already considering stopping the whole sugar baby business. I was genuinely tired of dealing with way older men. Despite the financial incentives, I wanted more from life, so I paused. And Yemi came along; he was funny and good looking. He worked as an investment banker. Even though he was not sugar daddy rich, he was still able to take care of me. I decided to give love a chance. I wanted to join all those people online that post nonsense pyjamas pictures online during Christmas.

We officially became an item when Covid arrived. I was

so in love with him and the vibe that we had that I became a proper *mumu*. Like I left my hostel to move in with him. Everything was going great, we were in our own little world. He had even teased marriage a few times.

Then I caught him in a threesome with two of my friends. Women who had their own partners. One was married, in fact. Well, not anymore – I heard her husband caught her cheating on him with his business partner. Like my blood boils when I think that I let that man fuck me without a condom! Do you know what that means for a girl like me? I have to really love you to let you enter me without a rubber.

Anyway, one of the babes filmed the threesome and sent it to me. I remember telling her Yemi could never cheat on me, and I think she just wanted to prove me wrong.

Men are strange! See how fine I am? I know I am skilful in bed, yet he chose to step out on me. When I confronted him about it, like he denied it, until I showed him the video. He started to accuse me and my friends of punishing him with 'revenge porn'. I deleted the video in his presence, packed my things and left his house for good.

I didn't want to go to Badagry to stay with my aunt, and my parents' place was out of the question. My mother sees me as a bank, so once I go home, all the outstanding bills are placed on my desk. I didn't need that kind of stress. So, I took some money, and sublet a place in Jacobs Mews Estate, Yaba, waiting for Covid to subside and university to resume.

While staying there, I met a girl called Sophie, who invited me on a 'strictly by invitation' cruise party on a boat. It was at that party that I met Njoku.

The whole thing was organised by a popular oil tycoon to celebrate his watch collection; he had just purchased a one-of-a-kind, diamond-studded Rolex and he wanted to show it off. You get? Babes at the party said the watch cost nearly a million dollars. Just imagine? Person carry a whole village salary put *am* for hand.

I am sure you know the tycoon, the one who has many petrol stations, and is always buying fancy cars for his children . . . Don't include his name, please, or he may sue you.

Anyway, Njoku and I met at that party, and within a week, he was chasing me hard and wooing me with gifts. I needed to get over Yemi, and I had heard from Sophie that Njoku was a money bag. So, I let myself fall for him. You have seen the pictures online; I know he looks like a possessed dog in the photos, but in person he was cute. Unlike during Covid, when Yemi and I were always together, Njoku gave me enough space. It was a pretty healthy relationship.

Once I agreed to be his babe, he got me the place in House Twenty-One Estate, and a car. I had always dated rich men, but meeting Njoku, I realised there are different levels of wealth. I was with him and his friend one day when they all bought a Mercedes-Maybach each to celebrate their club winning the championship league. One time, he bought me a designer bag just to say thank you for an incredible blow job. I thought we were in love. I always think these men love me.

One day, six months into the relationship, we went to an event hosted by his company in Calabar. They were launching a new product in collaboration with his foreign partners. At this time, everyone knew I was his babe. After the launch, we had a small party in the hotel lobby. But I was tired, so I told him I was going upstairs to sleep.

He whispered into my ear, 'Baby, my friend wants you.' I pretended not to hear him and went upstairs.

The next morning, Njoku gave me the silent treatment. Like he refused to speak to me and when it was absolutely necessary to talk, he was monosyllabic. Finally, I asked what the problem was.

'I told you my friend Farouk wanted to sleep with you last night and you ignored me,' he whined.

'I don't understand. Why would your friend want to sleep with your babe?'

'Is it not just sex? Does it matter who does it to you?'

'I don't sleep around!'

'Juicy, please! We both know most of the ladies who came to that party on the boat where we first met are *ashewos*. So, what's the big deal? Besides, it's my best friend, it will be like just sleeping with me.'

'No way!'

He stormed out of our room and almost left me in Calabar.

Once we got back to Lagos, Njoku froze the credit cards he had given me and avoided me for nearly two weeks. Like, I was miserable, not because of the money but because I missed him. So, I agreed. Imagine that? I broke up with Yemi because he had a threesome with two of my friends, only to end up with a sugar daddy with weird cravings. I slept with his best friend, and we were good. I know I could have broken up with him, but I had gotten used to the life he provided, and I liked him.

A month after that, he asked me to sleep with his best friend again. We fought for like a week before I caved in. Soon, it became a regular request. And whenever I refused him, he would scream and call me different names, and start breaking things, like a toddler.

That was how the women in the estate came to know of our fights.

To stop the *wahala* with him, I decided to let him have his way. Once I had accepted the arrangement, the reason for our constant bickering changed; he started to pick on me for little things that I did and would fly into a rage whenever I was unreachable.

After sleeping with Farouk the second time, I just accepted that I was with two men. And Farouk – I am sure you know him, he is the son of that man that owns the bank, the one always posing on social media now – he too is rich and very well connected. I think the sex was good for him because he would come to see me whenever Njoku was away.

We started to do our thing on the side. My truth was that I had now become a sugar baby for two powerful men. And I am not going to lie, it was nice because he was not as angry as Njoku. If Njoku bought me a Birkin, Farouk would buy me two in secret.

A year into the relationship, Njoku cloned my phone. I found out because he would say things that I knew I had only shared via text with a friend. When I told Farouk about my suspicions, he bought me another one.

One night Farouk said to me, 'Baby, can we stop using a condom? I know you use them with Njoku because he has told me. But I think what we have is really special, and I am falling for you. I want to feel you. Don't worry, I don't have any disease, and Njoku tells me you do a medical check-up every three months. I want you to know that if Njoku ever leaves you, you and I will be official.'

Like I was furious and told him I was not a pass-around.

He said, 'I know you are not. I just don't want to feel second to a man I know doesn't even like you like that. I too can buy you a house and give you the world.'

Eventually, I agreed, and we started sleeping together without using a condom.

Njoku must have started to suspect something was up with me and his best friend, because he stopped asking me to sleep with him.

Then the day before he died, I was with Farouk, and Njoku tracked my car. He had told me he was travelling for the week, so I left the estate to go stay with Farouk at the Southern Sun Hotel. I didn't know Njoku was setting a trap for me. He had me followed for a few days, and then he came to the hotel and had a public brawl with Farouk. When I refused to follow him after the fight, he left in a rage.

After things settled down at the hotel, Farouk and I both agreed that I would go to the university to sort some things out for my graduation, then go home to pack my belongings, get my passport, break up with Njoku and travel to Cape Town to meet him as he was going there for a work trip. He booked my flight before I left him at the hotel. Luckily, I had a visa to South Africa from when I'd travelled with Njoku for a business meeting.

While at the university, I received a call from one of the women in the estate, telling me that Njoku was there and making a ruckus. Without thinking, I went back just to calm Njoku down. When I walked in, I found Njoku dead. Blood everywhere. You know what happened after that – or you are going to eventually.

By the way, on Monday, I am going to court. I don't know if they told you.

TWENTY-TWO

Inefficient and Proud

FRIDAY

12.06 p.m.

The DPO stands over his table, laughing with some officers. As I walk in, he glances in my direction. 'Fine aunty. You are here today.' He licks his lips and arches his eyebrows. 'I hope you are okay.' I take a seat, ignoring the surprise on the faces of the officers, who all remain standing.

I ask coolly, 'Can I speak with you alone, sir?'

He nods and the officers leave, though I hear one hiss and murmur, 'This woman too do *sef*!'

Once we are alone, I let my mask slip a little, revealing my anger. 'Sir, who beat Juicy?'

He laughs as he sits. 'Madam, this is a police station. Anybody can beat anybody.'

'She has a black eye, sir.'

'Aunty, I don't know. I am not Juicy's bodyguard.'

I pound a fist on the table. 'Sir, this is a police station, these people are under your care—'

'Aunty!' He seizes his baton from the table and ominously raps it. 'This is not a daycare!'

On impulse, I stand to loom over him. 'Sir!'

He stands too. 'Do you think this is a private facility? Who are you to come here and question me?'

'I am her friend! And a concerned citizen.'

He raps his baton against the table again, this time a little harder. 'Oh, so you are a concerned citizen when it comes to an *ashewo*? Do you know what the police go through every day? Do you know the dangers we encounter? You are challenging me because a criminal got small beating?'

I lean forward to stare into his face, emboldened by anger. Shock registers in his eyes as he realises that I am not afraid of him. 'And who says she is guilty? Besides, what does that have to do with Juicy getting a black eye, sir?'

He makes a *tsk*-ing sound for a good ten seconds before answering, 'You care about Juicy but not the police, right? Madam, police no be human being *abi*?' He goes to the door and yells into the corridor, 'Mufu! Call Officer Rina and Fade! All of you, come to my office now!'

A hoarse voice responds immediately, 'Yes, sir!'

He walks back to sit, and signals for me to sit too. 'Aunty, sit down, please. Do you want to beat me?'

A minute later, three officers scurry in; two females and

one male arrange themselves in a straight line. Without looking at them, he says, 'Rina, tell me what happened to you last month?'

One of the female officers responds, 'An offender used his shoes to slap me, sir!'

'And?'

'My ear swell, sir.'

'Thank you. Fade, what happened to you two weeks ago?'

'An offender rubbed her own shit on my uniform and face, sir.'

'And?'

'She kicked me in the belly.'

'Mufu, what happened to you last year?'

The male officer shakes his head as if the memory of the event is still too heavy for him to carry. 'They shoot me for back, sir, and they leave me for bush. The boys that I tried to arrest over stolen vehicle.'

The DPO addresses me again. 'Aunty, brutality happens every day both in and outside of a police station. To civilians and police officers. I can't control it all.' He dismisses the officers with the wave of his baton. The silence after their departure is deafening, and I fiddle with my bag for a few seconds as he taps the baton lazily on the desk. Waiting.

Finally, I look up at him.

'I am sorry, sir.' I genuflect to show my remorse.

His lower lip drops, and a smile slowly spreads across his

face. '*Ahn ahn*, madam, you are too big to be kneeling. It's okay.' He moves around his desk quickly to help me up and I smell the beer on his breath. He lets his hands linger on my arms, drawing them slowly down to my hands, which he then holds in his own rough palms. 'You and Juicy are very beautiful. Nothing should be touching you. I was not around during the fight. I for stop *am*.'

I smile and edge my way out of his hold a little. He leans against his desk, facing me. 'Don't worry, I will take care of her going forward. Nothing will happen to her again. It's just that the girl is very, very stubborn. But no problem, I will treat her like my sister now.' He smiles and licks his lips.

'Thank you, sir. Let me be going, I have a meeting in another hour.' I take a step back and head to the door. Once I am at the entrance, I turn. 'I will be sure to tell Senator Yele that you have been very kind to me, sir.'

His face hardens briefly, then he breaks into deep, throaty laughter. 'Yes, my madam. Please tell my *oga* that I have been kind to you.'

TWENTY-THREE

The Other Sugar Daddy

FRIDAY

4.15 p.m.

Who is this Farouk?

The internet would have you believe that the man is a saint. In every article about him, every interview, he mentions his family. He has no social media footprint, only a website where he keeps a squeaky-clean image as a well-known philanthropist with his wife and two children – a son and a daughter. I guess that explains why he hasn't tried to help get Juicy out of jail. How could she have been so gullible to believe any of these men loved her?

I put on my Google notification for news about him.

Perhaps asking Yele for help will make my search easier, but I am not ready to pay for the consequences of that request.

I sit and write until the alarm goes off. Time to visit another neighbour.

As I walk to House Twelve, my tummy starts to feel funny. I ignore it and tap the doorbell.

'It's open.'

I walk inside and there is a woman standing there, already naked, her clothes piled by her feet. She is smiling. My jaw drops momentarily.

'Good evening, ma, is everything okay?' I ask.

She laughs. 'What is the code, dear?'

Oh, wow. How did she know I was coming?

'Juicy says—'

'It's enough,' she interjects. 'They told me you are collecting secrets about that day. You are a writer, yes?'

'I am but I am not writing about this, it is for—' I'm mid-sentence when the lights go out. I am grateful for the darkness. It gives me some time to think. *Which secret am I going to share with this woman now?* The generator comes on. The lights flicker and then still. I remove my clothes, slowly stealing glances at her.

Is that a mirror behind her? Why does this woman have mirrors everywhere?

Once I am naked, I see my reflection in the mirror closest to the door. I'm confronted by the sight of my left breast, which is starting to bow to life's pressures. I can see all my imperfections glaring back at me. She set this up deliberately.

She looks at me. 'My dear, do you work out?'

'Huh?'

'Do you go to the gym?'

'Sometimes.'

'You need to commit to it, dear. Your tummy has tendency to be big. It is not big yet. But I like your shape, and you are very beautiful. Just this tummy. Fix it!'

I keep my eyes on her face, but I don't miss her bingo wings, or how her chin triples when she speaks.

I don't have time to be telling this mummy she needs the gym more than me.

Again, there is something familiar about her face that I can't place. Was she a neighbour from my last house? Have I seen her at a reading? I stand there in my bare skin, waiting for her to speak.

Her gaze travels between my legs. 'I like the way you shave. Is that a V or an M? *Ahn ahn*, see style o,' she says.

I don't answer this. She laughs, looks at herself in the mirror, then says, 'Okay. Go on. I am listening.'

'*Ehn*?'

'My dear, what is the secret? The agreement we have is secret for secret now.'

'Why don't we get dressed and go to the backyard?' I suggest.

She shakes her head. 'I go to sleep at nine, and my children will soon come home from their swimming lesson. Say what you want now, and dress later. Let's hurry, please.'

I take a deep breath before speaking. 'I am an orphan.'

She stares at me, waiting. 'And?'

'Most people think my parents are alive because I created another personality online.'

She looks at me, intrigued. 'You are quite interesting. I like that.' She walks over and leans into my left ear, whispering, 'I am a whistleblower. All of my past relationships have been with high-profile men, and I am the one who blows the whistle on them once the relationship ends. They are all into some sort of crime, you know these men now, some do scam, others do politics. Once they leave me, I blow whistle on them. That way I earn as I mend my broken heart!' She tilts her head to gauge my response. I keep my expression blank although my tummy is starting to quake again. She leans back in. 'My ex rented this place for me, then broke up with me eight months later, I blew whistle on him o. Mad man, he was questioned for nearly six months over a deal he closed with a foreign company to sell vaccines.' She chuckles. 'The man I am seeing now is as clean as a whistle. But he is also very stingy, so I plan to incriminate him and blow the whistle after.' She laughs, darkly. 'Don't worry, all of my children are not from the men I have blown whistle on, I used different sperm donors for them. International ones, all my children are mixed. Fine fine *oyinbo* children.'

Okay, I can't hold it in anymore . . .

I rush out, looking for a toilet. Her voice guides me, 'It's on your left.' I run in and empty my lunch into the sink. I rest my head on the side. After a few seconds, a warm hand taps the nape of my neck. The woman has now made herself decent, in a red satin robe.

'Now to Juicy's secret. I was the one who cut the body up, the day Juicy killed her sugar daddy. So those pictures with her beside the body, *na* me do the chopping.'

I turn to the sink to relieve my belly again. This time nothing comes out.

She motions for me to sit on the toilet, and hands me my dress. 'You have more women to visit before your story is complete. You need to make your mind strong. Are you not the one who wants to help Juicy?'

She starts to clean the sink, rinsing it thoroughly. Once she finishes, she smiles at me. 'I will give you some time to get dressed. I hope you are no longer feeling nauseous.'

'No, thank you.'

As soon as she leaves, I put on my clothes. When I step out of the bathroom and I hear her singing, I follow the voice.

'*Kwere ogadiri dinma. Ekwere na* Jesus, *ogadiri dinma.*'

She is in the kitchen, chopping vegetables, and there are periwinkle snails soaking in a transparent plastic container beside the chopping board. Without missing a beat, she says, 'My dear, will you eat something? You poured out all your food in my bathroom.'

'No, thank you, ma.'

'Okay o.' She looks at me with her eyebrows raised.

'Thank you. Let me be on my way.'

She responds, 'Don't worry about Juicy. *Ashewo* no *dey* die for Lagos. Once everyone is done being angry at her, we will get her out. I just hope you are not writing a book about this.'

'No, I am not writing a story. I just want to find out who killed Njoku and what happened that day.'

'Hmm, and how is that your business? Anyway, if you *are* writing a book, change my name *biko*. And close the door behind you.'

I leave through the back door because I can hear her children screaming as they rush in through the main entrance. When I get home, I lie down on the floor in the front hall, my quaking tummy against the cold tiles. Slowly, I drift into sleep. My dreams are filled with Bawa, and the life she used to have.

TWENTY-FOUR

Weekend Aches

SATURDAY

8.25 a.m.

I drag myself out of bed in the morning. The ache in my stomach has disappeared, but the reality of Juicy's life and the society we live in weighs heavy on my mind. As I prepare to start writing again, I read the email from Susan that came in on Friday.

Dear Ara,

Congratulations again on your Women's Prize for Fiction nomination! Very exciting news . . . A feminist organisation reached out to us, hoping to partner with you to do some readings in the US. We have forwarded it to your PR agency. We would love for you to do this and will be working with Dotun to coordinate so that you can work it into the US leg of your book tour.

I hear a major streamer is looking at acquiring the film rights for your first three books. They are still speaking with your agency, but I am sure Dotun will let you know soon.

Hope writing is going well?

Talk soon,

Susan

I write back:

Dear Susan,

Wow, all of this sounds exciting!!!

Let's get it.

Very best,

Ara

The morning passes quickly as I bury myself in writing. It's as if the words were waiting to pour out of me. I play Juicy's recording, make some notes in my notepad, and then get back to writing. I take a break only when the alarm buzzes on my phone to prepare lunch – fried yam and corned beef sauce. After eating, I dive back into Juicy's world.

~

Evening comes with a sense of lethargy, prompting me to take a break. I scroll through my social media accounts. The first post that captures my attention is a frame of Njoku's wife, Edith, who recently gave a viral interview to Daddy Cold, a notoriously controversial journalist. I click to watch.

She is in a black *boubou*, her hair tucked into a black beret, and her eyes sunken as if grief is eating her from within. The infamous journalist wears a rumpled rust-coloured shirt.

PAPA COLD Sorry about your loss, ma.

EDITH Thank you.

PAPA COLD Now, I understand that you and your husband had been separated for some time, so many people are of course wondering why his death has hit you so hard.

EDITH We might have been separated, but he was still my children's father, the only love of my life, and I have not said this before, but we were in the process of reconciling.

PAPA COLD Tell us more about that.

EDITH (sniffing, her eyes starting to water) No marriage is perfect, and men cheat. We all know that. Nigerian men are who they are, but before that girl decided to butcher my husband up like suya, we had started going to church together again. We were even planning on seeing a marriage counsellor.

I pause the video to read the comments. They are tearing Juicy to pieces. I go back to press play.

PAPA COLD Really? There are marriage counsellors in Nigeria? I thought that was the job of religious leaders in this country. Pastors are also therapists here.

EDITH No, Njoku and I knew we needed professional help. (Sniffs again, a tear drops.) Njoku was willing to work on our marriage. We have three kids together.

PAPA COLD Have you seen the murderer since then?

EDITH Yes, I go to the station every day to ask her why she did this. Why? She's not the first person to have a sugar daddy. Why kill him? We have her in police custody in Oshòdì, so she is not going anywhere.

She starts to cry.

The interview has generated a lot of negative press online for Juicy. Bloggers are coming up with conspiracy theories and influencers are taking advantage of her popularity, using her as a conversation topic for their get-ready-with-me videos. Two years ago, a popular influencer named a candle collection after an #EndSARS slogan. I remember being stunned that a Nigerian, who just happens to live abroad, would seek to capitalise on the pain that still bleeds red in the country. Now, with this Juicy's matter, I expect that in the next two months, another Nigerian abroad will do an HBO special about her, when it is too late for Juicy, to line their pockets.

Why am I the only one seeing that there's a story and a person behind the headlines, rather than just feeding off internet-based gossip?

I play another viral video featuring Montana, Juicy's friend from school, who has also given a TV interview while in Dubai.

'We were close, but I never knew she was capable of murder,' she says tearfully to the interviewer.

All these people are wrong about Juicy. But how do I tell them?

If I tell Juicy's story in a book, how long will it take before it comes out, before people can read it? African publishers will publish within a year, the West will take a little longer, then I have to wait for influential human rights activists that can help her to read the book.

If I pay some of the bloggers to tell another side of the story, would that sway the public's opinion? From the number of hashtags popping up across all the platforms, it is clear Juicy is popular with most Nigerians at home and abroad. But for every second that she remains locked up, her life loses value.

I drift off on the sofa while watching social media destroy the poor girl.

MOTIVE

TWENTY-FIVE

Another Day, Another Palaver

MONDAY

11.06 a.m.

As I drive past Victoria Island, I see a small crowd gathering around a girl in a blonde wig, black shirt and blue skinny jeans. She has a placard that reads, 'I need a boyfriend.' Onlookers are taking pictures of her as she strikes different poses.

I hope she goes viral, I think. *So Juicy can rest.*

Once I get to the station car park, I see the DPO stepping out of the building with two other officers.

'Good morning, sir,' I call out to him from my car.

He breaks into a smile. 'Ah, sister. Juicy is in the van, going to court. She didn't tell you?'

'I know, sir. Can I come? I don't mind taking you there, sir, and bringing you back. I hope you are not still angry with me over last week's incident?'

'*Haba*, you have apologised.' He scratches his head and

licks his lips for a few seconds, before answering. 'Okay, to show you I am not angry anymore, I will let you drive me.'

'Thank you, sir.'

The DPO jumps into the passenger seat beside me, and the officers take the back seat as we head to the court.

A few minutes into the drive, the DPO starts to inspect the vehicle, opening every compartment including the glove box. He smiles when he sees some dollar notes. '*Ahn ahn*, madam, you are a big woman o.'

'My *Oga*, we bless God. How come Juicy is already going to court, sir? Is it not too soon?'

He laughs. 'My sister, you too like this Juicy *sha*. You sure say she no be your sister? Well, this is Nigeria, she messed with a powerful family, and they can make things happen. They are even trying to move her to Kirikiri Maximum Security Prison.'

'Hmm.'

He turns the air conditioning vent to get more air coming his way. His oniony stench soon fills the car. The officers in the back start to doze off. The DPO continues. 'Juicy has to ride in the official bus. She is a criminal,' he says, as if he can tell I wish I was driving Juicy myself.

Once we are seated in the courtroom, I can see people taking pictures and recording videos of Juicy, who is already in the witness box. In the early hours of this morning, Dotun sent me a few clips on WhatsApp.

> I know you said to leave you alone, but I just wanted you to know your neighbour is trending and someone is already trying to set up a hair business so that girls can have full edges like her on their head! Watch and laugh. By the way, the film rights for your three books have received a really juicy offer. I'll keep you posted.

A woman comes into the courtroom prompting me to close my phone. Her presence is immediately the source of much attention, made worse by the way she is looking at Juicy with disdain. As she gets closer, I recognise her as Edith, wife of the deceased. She looks like a much older version of the woman I've seen online. Her husband's death has started to take its toll.

I shift my attention to the lawyer assigned to defend Juicy, a short man with a receding hairline. He walks over to speak with his client.

As the court clerk addresses the noisy crowd, Juicy smooths her hair repeatedly, and keeps her gaze down. The bruise on her face has turned green. I hope she looks up so she can see me smiling at her.

'Court rise!' the clerk announces, causing the room to fall silent.

The judge walks in. He looks overfed and shiny with avarice. He stifles a yawn.

'Can the defendant and the prosecutor please approach the bench?'

Someone sits down beside me and the smell that emanates from them forces me to shuffle along. It's hard to breathe, but I have to be here for Juicy. I look back at her and this time she is also looking at me. She mouths *thank you*, and I respond, *you are welcome*.

The court appearance was for Juicy's lawyer to seek bail, but it is not granted. As soon as this is decided, I send Ezu, my lawyer that Dotun introduced to me when I signed with her agency, an email.

Hi Ezu,

How are you? It's been a while. I hope you are keeping well?

So, I have a case I need your help with urgently, please. I am not sure if this is your area of the law or if someone else can handle it at your firm. Can you please look into this girl's case? Her lawyer is not great. I have attached everything I know about her.

I stop to take a picture of Juicy so he can see her bruised face for himself. I attach the photo and send it.

When I get outside, the DPO and his officers are standing by my car, chatting about Juicy and the unfortunate turn of events. I drop them back at the station, reminding him that

I will be back the next day. As I circle out of the car park, one of the officers runs out.

'Aunty! Stop o! Juicy will talk to you. She says she wants you to come now.'

TWENTY-SIX

Juicy's Confession III

MONDAY
2.40 p.m.

Thank you for today.

Me I have accepted that my mother and father had no business being parents. Useless people! I think it's the case for most children growing up in Nigeria. But I at least expected my mother to show up in court today! After all, I always sent some of the money I made being a sugar baby back to her. I was hoping my aunt would come as well. I don't have high expectations of my father – the man has been drunk for as long as I can remember. I learned to recognise the smell of *Kai Kai* on him at a very young age. I have given half of everything I made over the years to my family, and I don't regret it. I just wish my parents could be better. You know, it wouldn't hurt if they stood by me or even sent someone to visit me. But it is what it is. We move!

As I said, those women on the estate came into my life through Njoku. One of those nights when we had been fighting, I stepped out to smoke and calm down a bit, and one of them was at the gate. I didn't really say anything to her, but she could tell I was upset. She smoked with me and invited me to her house. I didn't go at first because I wasn't sure how Njoku would feel if I made friends with the neighbours. But a week later, he and I fought again. So, I went to visit her, and gradually, she introduced me to some of our other neighbours. We bonded over our experiences with men. We all leaned on one another. So, I am a little sad that they could not even come to see me in jail. It is only you – the neighbour I never knew before – who is here for me during this time. From what we saw in court today and the way my lawyer is acting, I am not likely to get out of here on bail. So, can you please go to Houses Fifteen and Four by ten p.m. and twelve p.m.?

TWENTY-SEVEN

Freedom

MONDAY

11.37 a.m.

'How do you know which houses I should go to and at what time?' I ask after placing the recorder in my bag. Juicy smiles.

'I have known these women for a long time. This is how we do things.'

'What does that mean?'

'We designated these times to visit one another. Especially when we have to trade secrets or talk about our men.'

'So, this has happened before?'

'Writer, focus on your story. Don't worry about anything else. If time permits, we will talk about that.'

'The internet says you were in a tussle with Njoku before he died. Have you been physical with him? Did you hit him in the past?'

'To protect myself, I would ward off his blows sometimes, especially with my face, that is my money maker.'

'Oh.'

'The internet is full of nonsense. Njoku was violent and I sometimes fought back. Finish.'

I can tell that is all she will share so I make another suggestion. 'If you like, I can help you contact your family.'

Her face breaks into a twisted smile. 'My mother and aunty know where to find me. I have sent them messages with the DPO's phone.'

'Let me try at least. With all of them. They may help your case. Let's give them one last chance.'

'Bring me a piece of paper.' She scrawls the addresses and phone numbers on the sheet for me.

On my way home, the clouds overhead hang loosely as though they might drop down at any moment on the road that leads up to the bridge. The sun has dipped below the horizon, leaving a splash of colour across the sky. I wonder if Juicy will ever get to enjoy freedom again. I want to tell her that I understand her pain, that pain is a universal language most women speak fluently, but I think my silence is a better companion for her than my words during this time.

As I drive through Ozumba Mbadiwe, I see a blind man who is singing and playing a guitar at the junction. The sound of his solo performance filters through the mounted speaker beside him. His sonorous voice has captured the attention of some passers-by, who are taking videos and dropping money into the basket in front of him.

This is the kind of content that should go viral, not Juicy's story.

Once I get home, I firmly tuck the sheet with Juicy's family's contacts on it in my wallet, and then I go upstairs to take a nap.

All too soon, my phone buzzes, and I check the time. It is ten minutes to ten.

Time to go learn more about Juicy and my murderous neighbours.

~

I knock at the door of House Fifteen and wait. I hear footsteps approaching rapidly. It sounds as if the person on the other side is struggling with the keys. A voice stutters, 'I'm so sorry, this door is jammed.' After a minute, the door opens. It's Burqa.

Oh no!

Her face lights up as if I am an old friend.

'Writer! What a pleasant surprise. Can I help you?'

'Juicy says *ashewo*.' The light in her eyes immediately goes out, replaced by a blank expression.

'What do you want?'

'I want to rent a secret.'

'Why?'

'Juicy wants to know what happened before she got home that day.'

'Come in quickly.' She hurries me in and is already taking her clothes off.

'But you acted like you didn't even know Juicy last Saturday, when we first spoke,' I say as I start to undress.

'I don't know her. She is not my family.'

'Hmmm.'

Her face is fully revealed as she takes off her burqa. *Wow!* My eyes travel from her lustrous, curly black hair to her pointed nose. Her perfect figure and taut tummy mock my not-so-flat one. I take in her beauty in gulps. *This woman is stunning! Is it me or does she look a little like Juicy?* She moves closer to me.

'Why are you really doing this? Are you writing something on Juicy?'

'No.'

Fuck. Maybe I shouldn't lie to her.

'I don't know, to be honest. I just want to find out how a man was killed in this estate, and we didn't know about it. Sorry, I mean *I* didn't know.'

She smiles at me, revealing her beautifully straight, milk-white teeth. 'You have only been here for eight months, Writer, and you are not particularly friendly. How can you possibly know what is going on in the estate when you lock yourself away in the house all the time?'

'You are right. But that still doesn't explain how a man was killed here, and no one knew about it. Going by how much I have found out ever since it happened, I was right to be suspicious.'

'Hmmm.'

We dress again, but she leaves her burqa off and touches my arm.

'If it is okay with you, let's just talk here. That whole backyard business makes me uncomfortable.'

'Okay. So—'

She raises her hand. 'I'll go first. I killed my husband because he gave one of our babies to a business partner who took the child's eyes out.' She clutches her chest and whispers a short phrase in Arabic before she continues. 'When we got married, we were so poor. I ran away with him because I didn't want to marry the old man my family had offered me to. So when my husband, a young trader, asked me to run off with him to another village, I did. But we needed money desperately. One of his friends told him we could get rich quickly if we were willing to do a certain kind of business. It was a dark kind of business indeed. We would have to sell our babies to be raised as professional beggars on the streets.'

Excuse me?

'Those beggars you see on the roadside, some of them are professionals. They beg for a living. They or their employers inflict deliberate injuries so that they can more successfully seek alms. I didn't want to do it, but things were really tight, and I finally agreed. The first time I got pregnant, we had triplets. I wanted to keep one, but my husband would not allow it. We sold the babies and within a week, we were able to rent a flat. Do you want to sit down?' she asks, looking up at me.

No. I want to get out of here, ehn?

'I am fine,' I say instead.

'Anyway, after weeping every day for the next month, I decided on a new strategy. I thought that if we got enough money, we could go get our children back. So, I started getting pregnant every year. Luckily, I am very fertile. And I always seem to give birth in twos or threes. All in all, I have had ten babies, and I know where they all are. Using the money from selling my sweet babies in this trade, we became so rich . . . ' She slips to the ground, and I lower myself to sit beside her. 'The last time I got pregnant, I thought, ah, these ones I can keep. They were a set of twins. I told my husband, and he agreed. After all, we didn't need the money anymore. Do you know that bastard sold the babies straight from the clinic? After I had healed and was able to track them down, I found out the buyer was different from the others and had taken their eyes. I was furious and disgusted with myself. I was even more disgusted with my husband. That night when I got home, I poisoned him, watched him convulse to death and disposed of his body two days later. Then I moved to Lagos.'

'Oh, this didn't happen here?'

'No, it was in Kano.'

I feel as if I've been punched in the gut, hearing this story. I have no idea what to say except:

'I am sorry.'

She takes my hand. 'Now to Juicy's secret. I was there that night when Njoku died. Juicy is not the killer.'

'Why didn't you call the police?'

'I'm sure you understand why I avoid the police. I can't afford to attract their attention.' She stands up and I do the same. 'I just want my children. I have all this,' she gestures around her, 'but no children.' She starts to cry again. I don't say anything and shed a few tears myself. We exchange a hug before I leave.

At the door, I realise that I didn't have to tell Burqa any of my secrets.

~

Long Legs lives in House Four!

I don't know why I didn't remember this when Juicy told me to go there earlier. I live in House Five, so I should have clocked that this would be my next-door neighbour again. I check my phone: it's quarter to midnight. I can't sit at home, so I walk around the garden where we had the meeting on Sunday. The dim overhead lamps guide my walk with their lazy illumination.

Why did all these women pretend not to know Juicy when the estate manager announced the murder? What secret does Long Legs have to tell me about Juicy?

My watch buzzes at midnight. I walk to House Four and knock. The door swings open.

'Come in, Writer.'

Kai. This woman freaks me out.

I walk in and she is already naked, seated on a couch in her tropical-themed living room.

'Code word?' she asks.

'Code word?'

She squeals. 'I love how exciting this is. Say the code word!'

This woman is bloody annoying.

'Juicy says *ashewo*?'

She arches her brow. 'Is that a statement or a question?'

'A statement.'

'Then say it properly.'

This freak.

'Juicy says *ashewo*.'

'What do you want?'

'I want to rent a secret.'

She smirks. 'Why?'

I roll my eyes before answering. 'Juicy wants to know what happened that day—'

'So, this girl really sent someone to find out what

happened before she got here that day? She is so forward. How hard is it to stay in police custody, *ehn* Writer? Have you ever been arrested for writing about what is not your business? Tell me, have you ever been to jail?'

I ignore her and start to undress instead. I take my trousers off. She stops me with a guffaw when I try to take off my blouse. 'Please! I don't need to see you completely naked! I know the rules so I can bend them.'

She walks over to me and takes my hand. I resist her pull. She stops to look at me. I smile.

'Please, let me put my trousers back on. Is that not the arrangement? To be fully clothed as we share secrets.'

'Fuck that. Follow me.' She leads me to the backyard and beckons me to sit down on the two-seater, then walks around me for nearly a minute. I follow her with my eyes.

I hope this aunty is not planning anything because I will kill her before she kills me.

Then she comes to sit beside me. 'Writer, this your *nyash* is too big. Please don't break my chair.'

What is this woman's problem?

I turn to look at her, moving away as far as the two-seater will allow me, so there's no chance of us brushing up against one another.

'I am sorry. I will sit with half an ass if you want,' I offer.

She catches the sarcastic note and hisses. I hide a smile. She snaps her fingers. 'Okay. Your secret first?'

I look away from her as I speak. 'I think you should go first. You did just say you can bend the rules.'

She relaxes into the chair, spreading her legs slightly. 'Well, I killed my father. He was sleeping with my husband. For four years! How do you take your child's heart and break it? That's how! Sadly, I didn't kill my ex, but I hope he dies soon.' She laughs a little. 'He knows I had something to do with my father's death. He just can't pin the murder on me. So, to punish me, he cut me off financially and took our two children, leaving me to fend for myself. You can't imagine how hard it was to go from spending almost a million naira in a week to being on the street with no means to feed. Thankfully, I met someone who changed my life, and he moved me here. Sadly, that didn't last.' Her eyes start to well up, and the light from the bulb above us catches the gleam.

I need to leave this house before I start feeling sorry for her.

'And Juicy's secret?' I ask.

'If you are not going to share a secret of your own, I want you to pay my rent next year,' she says unexpectedly.

'Excuse me?'

'If you want me to tell you her secret, and trust me you do, you will pay my rent next year. Are you not a successful writer? I have looked you up. I did not know African literature was selling like that.'

Okay, Ara, you have come this far, you can bribe her.

I turn to her.

'I won't pay your rent, but I can add a hundred thousand naira to whatever it is.' She eyes me and I hear her call me cheap under her breath.

'I saw who killed Njoku.'

I feel myself getting hot. My tummy is starting to turn again.

'Who was it?'

'That's enough for now.' She turns to me, an angry expression on her face. 'Why do you care about Juicy, for *gawd's* sake? Is she your sister?'

'Tell me who killed Njoku.'

'I can't say who, but she lives on the estate. She had an affair with him.' She lets out a small squeal, as if talking about murder excites her. 'Alright, I will tell you one more secret for free. I was also the one who called the police on Juicy. I hate the girl. Too bad you can't tell anyone. Shut the door on your way out.' She gets up, dismissing me.

I try to stand up but everything suddenly goes dark.

~

'I can't believe you fainted because of this Juicy business.'

My vision starts to clear, and I weakly try to sit up. The figure speaking is clearer now. It is Long Legs and she looks annoyed.

'Is Juicy your sister?' She walks over to the television stand and picks up a cigarette. She's still wearing nothing.

Is this woman about to smoke? When I just fainted?

She speaks again after taking a drag. 'Listen, the whole country already thinks she is guilty. What does it matter if I tell you who killed Njoku? Have you seen what is happening on social media? They fucking hate her. Married women, especially.'

'Can I have some water?' I ask as I reach down to pick up my trousers from the floor.

'Aunty, you live opposite me. Please, get up and go home,' she shoots back.

I check my watch. It is one a.m. I stand but have to sit again immediately. My ears are ringing. I see Long Legs looking at me through the cigarette smoke.

'Shit. Now I have to wear your clothes for you,' she says as she walks over and helps me into my trousers. I lean against her as we walk out of her house and over to my door. I check for the key in my pocket. Once the door is open, she turns away and I nearly trip into the house.

She tosses her words at me as I struggle. 'I don't know why you need to help this girl or what your plan is. But I can tell you for free, this is not a fight you can win. People hate this girl. I will send you my account details. Send my hundred thousand naira today.'

I watch her butt cheeks jiggle furiously.

I can't believe she walked naked to my house and back.

TWENTY-EIGHT

Farouk

TUESDAY
9.40 a.m.

My phone's vibration wakes me up.

I hold it up to see a Google alert. Apparently, Farouk is hosting a seminar for business executives in Abuja on Wednesday. On his website, it says it had been advertised for nearly three months prior, but it was called off due to Njoku's death. However, in the spirit of honouring his friend, he has decided to have the seminar to help build promising entrepreneurs.

The Early Bird tickets are priced at three hundred thousand naira and are already closed. Late Bird tickets are going for five hundred thousand. The event – which will run for two days from ten a.m. to six p.m. daily – promises to introduce small business owners to a network of individuals whose joint net worth is over twenty million dollars.

Aren't philanthropists supposed to give everything for free, including knowledge?

I book the earliest flight which is for seven a.m. the next day.

TWENTY-NINE

Abuja

WEDNESDAY
10.12 a.m.

Transcorp Hilton reeks of Oud and every supposedly expensive perfume.

The path to the 'Winner By Force' seminar hall is lined with posters of Farouk and some other people that I assume are giants in their fields. I pass the time watching documentaries on my phone about women who kill their partners, as the various experts share stories on how they worked very hard to become multi-billionaires in a country that is corrupt and poor.

Two hours into the training, we break for tea. Farouk is talking to some trainees, but I see his eyes dart to me a few times, his gaze falling to my lips each time. The make-up artist who met with me in the hotel's bathroom to work her magic with my blank canvas had over-lined my lips, making them pouty and glossy. The purple suit I am wearing is cinched at the waist with a belt (I read somewhere that purple is his favourite colour), and my hot comb-straightened hair dances around my shoulders.

I walk over to join them.

'And what business do you do, madam?' he turns to me and asks with a smile.

'I export palm oil overseas, sir,' I lie without batting an eyelid.

'Ah, that's interesting. Stop to talk with me during lunch.'

A few of the people stare at me so I scurry away to my seat at the far end of the hall.

After the first round of training, we break for lunch. Farouk walks over to me. 'Please join me for lunch, Ara.'

I nearly trip.

~

'I recognised you from your last book, which I enjoyed thoroughly,' he says as the waiters bring an assembly line of dishes to our very long dining table. 'I hope you don't mind. I tend to nibble so I like to eat from everything the kitchen has before I make a choice.'

I nod, hoping some moisture has found its way into my throat.

'So, to what do I owe the honour, Ara?'

'I am here on behalf of Juicy.' He raises his hand to

stop the waiter approaching our table. The man bows and turns back.

He smiles. 'How is she? I have not been able to see her.'

'She is in police custody.'

He wipes his hands with a hot towel, arching his brow toward the dishes on the table.

'I am not hungry. Thank you,' I say in response to the silent invitation. He smiles.

'My personal chef, who I brought in from Calabar, made these meals. Please don't insult him by not eating.'

'Okay.'

I sanitise my hands as he serves me a plate of fisherman soup, and *eko*.

'I hope you like *eko*, I love it.'

'I do. It's my comfort food.'

He winks at me. 'I know. I read it in one of your interviews. I had them go into town to buy it once I spotted you in the hall.' He takes a teaspoon of everything onto his plate. 'I am aware that Juicy is in police custody. How is she?'

I watch as he starts to sample the dishes like a child. 'She is doing her best,' I respond.

'Good.'

I take a bite of my food. He smiles. 'Delicious, right?'

'Yes.'

'So, what do you want from me, Ara?'

'I wondered if you could give me any information about Juicy – just anything that would help her case.'

He stops eating. 'How do you know Juicy exactly?'

'She is my neighbour.'

'Ah, that's interesting. And you are writing about her?'

'I am trying to help her—'

He clears his throat. 'She didn't kill Njoku.'

'How do you know that?'

'Njoku had her on a leash. I think she may have even loved him. Poor girl.' He shakes his head as he continues his food tasting. 'Whoever killed Njoku is the one that set her up. The man was a woman beater and abuser.'

'Yet he was your best friend?'

'If I throw out every friend who beats or abuses women, I'll be left with no one. Most men I know secretly hate women.'

'Can you at least testify on her behalf?'

He looks at me, his face wrinkles into a frown. 'I am a married man. I simply cannot do that.'

'You were also sleeping with her.'

'Yes, I was, but I can't risk my marriage for Juicy. I am sorry.'

'I don't know how to help her.'

'I can give you some money to help her case. She might be in jail, but that doesn't mean she should be uncomfortable. Once the media scrutiny dies down, we will find a way to help her leave the country—'

'I think testifying about their relationship will help. She has a life here. She is supposed to be graduating soon.'

He gets up abruptly. 'I need to get back to my training. We can talk some more over dinner, if you like. I love that purple on you. Very becoming.'

'Thank you.'

Once he leaves, I book the next flight out for six p.m. that evening and head straight to the airport.

THIRTY

Anger Ascending

THURSDAY
9.17 a.m.

Burqa is carrying a large grocery bag towards her house as I head out. She is looking straight ahead, but I call out to her anyway.

'Good morning. Do you need help? Where is Solomon?'

'No, it's fine. Thank you, Writer.'

She increases her pace as if she is scared that I will come and snatch it.

I throw my purse onto the passenger seat and drive out of the estate.

There is some smoke in the air around Oshòdì as I drive towards the station. I see a group of Okada riders putting out a fire. As I drive by, I can only hope that it is not another human being burning. Ten minutes later, I arrive at the station. Luckily, there is a free parking space right in front. I walk into the station and find it empty.

'Hello! Good morning?!' I call out. No one answers.

Where did they go? Do I just go through to Juicy, or should I sit and wait?

I hear voices from the cells.

Is today the first of May? Is it a holiday?

I walk up to the counter and past it. I make my way cautiously along the corridor and hesitate before passing the first cell.

Wait o. What if the detainees broke out and killed the officers?

I readjust the belt on my DVF wrap dress – a gift from Dotun to mark the achievement of being a three-time bestseller.

'I know you wouldn't buy this expensive piece for yourself. You are too stingy. This dress is worth three hundred dollars, so please wear it to a good place and take pictures,' she said as she pushed the gift bag into my hands.

I thanked her and hung the dress in my wardrobe, never intending to wear it. It looked too expensive, but today I wanted to offset my moodiness from the encounter with Farouk by looking extra nice.

Maybe I should send Dotun a picture now before these prisoners maul me.

'Madam! Why are you here?!' I see a group of police officers coming down the corridor. They're carrying bags of what must be the remains of their lunch, and some drinks.

'Madam, did you hear me?' The man who addressed me is walking faster towards me now, leaving the herd behind.

My heart starts to race. 'I am sorry. I was looking for—'

'So, you decided to come to the back by yourself? Who gave you authorisation?' he growls. He is right in front of me now. I can see the oil from the food he just ate around his thin lips. His peppery breath stings my eyes.

'I am sorry—'

'Dauda, she is from the boss so please let's not touch her. Let her go.' Another officer steps in to rescue me. My saviour is the female officer I met on the first day.

'*E* no mean. Na why she *dey* do anyhow,' he hisses and walks away.

'Madam, you *sef* you too *dey* do *oversabi*. Abeg, follow me,' she hisses at me.

I walk meekly behind her. She leads me to the usual spot. I see that Juicy is eating a piece of fish from the same place the officers have been for their lunch. At least they're feeding her. The bruise around her eye is now blackish.

'You have two hours,' the officer tells us.

'Okay, thank you.'

She leaves and I sit with Juicy, who continues to eat, ignoring me. She sucks noisily on a bone. *Have I upset her?* After a minute, she goes to wash her hands. 'These people can't even give me a tissue,' she says as she wipes her hands on the lower part of her overalls.

She sits for a moment before speaking. 'Why are you so interested in my story again? Where were you for two days? And please don't lie to me!'

'I had a few things to attend to outside Lagos.'

'And you don't think you should have informed me? Even the DPO says you didn't reach out.'

'I am sorry.'

'Why are you so interested in my story? Like are you bored?'

'You know I am a writer?'

She shakes her head furiously. 'No, I don't. Tell me something I don't know. So, Madam Writer, you want to use me as your next subject? You want to make money off me? Are you paying me for this story?!'

'I want to write about you. Will I be paid? Yes. But I am not doing it for the—'

'And you will make plenty of money off your neighbours and me, *abi*?' she says, hissing.

I have had it with this girl!

'That's what being paid means! But I am writing this book for myself, and for you. Not for the gain! For months, all I have felt is an urge to jump off a bridge. Trying to help you is the first time in a long time that I haven't wanted to end my own life. If I can tell your story and find at least one influential person who will read it and listen to what I am saying, maybe you won't rot in here! I thought you were fine with me writing about it. You said so yourself. Those women are not coming to save you. No one is. But I want to try. I have to. So please stop making this about money! Money is not the goal here!'

She stares at me, dumbfounded. She walks over to me, tries to touch my face, but I tilt my head, so she misses. She smiles and tries again. This time I let her.

'You are crying.'

I put a hand to my cheek. *Shit.* She wipes the tears off with her hands and goes back to sit on the sofa opposite me. 'I am sorry. I have been on edge since one of the women you met with called me. Like I didn't even know they could find a way to access me until one of the officers brought the phone to me. When I answered, all she said was you are not to be trusted.'

Let me guess. Long Legs.

'Who?' I ask.

She smiles and waves it off. 'Never mind.' She rests her head on the arm of the sofa.

'Listen, like I know older people don't like the sound of therapy—'

'I am not that old.'

'You are older than me at least.'

'True.'

She laughs. 'Ara, you may need therapy. No one this successful should want to jump off a bridge. Like if I had your life, I would be travelling the world. If I had time to discover a talent, you think I would be fucking married men?'

'You do have talents. You may even be a creative.'

She pats her hair. 'Hmmm. I hear you. *Sha* try therapy. Talk to someone.'

'Okay. I will.'

She crosses her legs. 'Since we started this, you have not asked me the most important question.'

'I haven't?'

'No.'

'What is the question?'

'Why are these women willing to tell you their deepest, darkest secrets?'

This is true. I didn't ask. But I assumed it was because the women also knew my secrets.

'Why?' I ask her.

She takes a deep breath and chuckles. 'Because secrets eat you up and if there is a listening ear to take the burden off you, without the mouth betraying you, you will tell. Talking to you has helped me stay sane in this place. Those women are the same. They are looking for someone who will carry their secrets and not share them with others.'

'But I am writing a book about them and their secrets . . . '

'No, you are writing a book that may or may not be about them. It depends on the women.'

'I see,' I say, though I don't see at all what she is getting at.

'Let us begin.'

I set my recorder down on the table and press the red button.

THIRTY-ONE

Juicy's Confession IV

All those women were once Njoku's mistresses.

I didn't want to tell you before. Like I myself figured it out a year into our relationship when I was complaining to one of them about him and she said, 'That's how he is. You have to accept that being a sugar baby, a little bit of your dignity dies each day. He is like that—' She stopped when she realised what she'd said. I didn't push it. I just started to do some research myself. I casually asked Farouk, who had a freer mouth when he'd had a drink or two.

'*Ehn hen* now, all his former babes are in that estate, but you're the only one he bought a house for, which is why I wanted to taste you too. That secret place in between your legs must be special if a man is buying you a house.'

So, the women were all brought into the estate by Njoku. Not at the same time, of course. The first woman I sent you to meet was also the first tenant in the estate. They were together for a year or so. I think he cycles through women as they age. Once you are close to thirty-five, he breaks up with you, but you are free to stay in the estate. The only thing is, he won't pay your rent anymore. He expects you'll find another lover to help with that if you want to maintain the same lifestyle. Or you can just leave, of course.

Like you have seen how comfortable our living situation is; no Lagos woman who has experienced that would choose to go back to the life she had before. Some eventually leave because paying rent on the Island is pure robbery. And not all sugar daddies are born equal.

Anyway, Njoku was one of the most important tenants and house owners in that estate. All the women in the estate are side chicks of big men in Nigeria.

Doesn't that mean you are also one of us?

THIRTY-TWO

Swipe Right

THURSDAY
12.30 p.m.

Tinder brought Yele into my life.

A few years ago, one of my Twitter followers mentioned that they had used the app for free hook-ups or to find companionship in their neighbourhood. I downloaded it and registered with the username *@Inemlovesya*. My profile picture was a photo of a girl sleeping on a pile of books, which I'd taken from some website. After blocking two perverts who messaged me only late at night, asking me to send them pictures of me licking my feet and various dirty objects, I decided to give the app one more try. His username was *@Yourdaddy* – an annoying pseudonym, but his bio had promise. He said he loved to read books in his spare time. Once we had both swiped right, he sent me a message suggesting that we meet. I had finished my writing target for that day and decided I could do with the free meal.

Two hours later, we met at Lagosia on Alexander Road, Ikoyi. Like me, he didn't look anything like his profile picture, which was a photo of an old man smoking a cigar. He was way better looking. At five foot eleven, he towered over me. He wore a blue face-cap, paired with a pink T-shirt and faded blue jeans. He smiled a lot, his goatee moving up and down as he spoke.

'I'm sorry if you didn't know what to expect. I didn't want you to find out who I am or what I look like and not show up.'

'That's okay. As you can see, I didn't use a real profile picture either.'

'Do you want to eat?'

'Yes, please.'

'You should try the local dishes here. They are really good.'

'Okay, thank you.'

After we'd ordered and were waiting for our meals to arrive, he told me he was a politician, was divorced from his wife, and that he liked drinking beer, which was why he ran every day to avoid getting a pot belly. I told him I was a teacher-turned-writer, and broke. The waiter brought his order: seafood okro and *eba*. The steam from the food made his face shiny.

'What kind of thing do you write?' he asked as he ate.

'Stories.'

'As in, children's stories, newspaper articles or what?'

'I write novels and short stories.'

'Ara . . . Ara . . . wait. I have seen that name on a book my daughter was reading – are you the girl that wrote—' I cut him off before he said it.

'Yes! Guilty.'

'How can you be broke? Your book is all over Lagos. You artists make a lot of people very happy. Surely with the success you've had, you must earn plenty?'

'It takes a minute before you can make money as a writer. I am not broke broke, but I am not rich either,' I responded, sipping slowly on my virgin mojito. 'I can't go back to my work as a teacher because the pay is also not great. And I want to focus on writing,' I told him.

'Didn't your book help make connections for you?'

'It did, but not enough to make steady money yet. I need to write, but if I get a nine-to-five, I won't be able to.'

'So, how do you survive?'

'I get by on my royalties till the next payment comes in. I can't do anything else. All I want to do is write books.'

He looked at me with pity and reached across the table to place his hands over mine. Another waiter brought the fisherman's soup and semolina I'd ordered, causing him to break away. I took my time to eat, despite the hunger gnawing at me. I wanted to make a good impression. After eating for some time, I broke the silence.

'Let's go to my house,' I said.

He arched his left brow. 'Why not mine?' he countered.

'Are you not a known senator?' I watched him scoop some okro into his mouth.

'You are a known writer too,' he said after he was done swallowing.

'Yes, but I am still at a stage in my career where I can get away with murder.' I winked at him.

'Okay,' he laughed, and beckoned to the waiter to bring the bill.

We left shortly after in a Porsche with tinted windows, and all through the trip, he kept looking at my lips and thighs. At my suggestion, we stopped at a twenty-four-seven pharmacy so I could get a morning-after pill and HIV test kits.

'If you are worried about me, I always use a condom,' he said before I got out.

'Can't be too safe. The test won't take more than thirty minutes, if it's alright with you.'

'It's fine.'

We waited by the pharmacy to take the tests.

'What would have happened if one of us was positive?' he asked after the result came out negative for both of us.

'Nothing. We would still be friends.'

We drove home in silence.

Once we got to my apartment, I turned to him. 'Please, whatever you do, don't bite my nipples.' Godsword had a thing for that, and I was uninterested in unnecessary tooth marks.

'Okay, ma,' he responded. I led him inside. My mattress was on the floor, close to the wall. I watched as he took off his clothes. He struggled with his trousers for a minute, then looked up at me. 'Are you not going to take yours off?' he asked.

'I'm just realising that it is my first time seeing a man in this apartment since I moved in.'

'Oh, do you want to go to a hotel?' he asked.

'No, it's fine.'

I took my clothes off and we laid on my mattress. The standing fan in the other corner of the room was the only sound in the room for a while. We both stared at the ceiling.

Suddenly he said, 'You don't have a sofa.'

'Huh?'

'You don't have a sofa or a bedframe,' he repeated.

'Not yet. I have more pressing expenses.'

'Okay.'

He leaned on his elbow to face me and traced my cleavage with his thumb.

'You are a very beautiful girl.'

'Thank you.'

Teasing each nipple with his mouth, he sucked gently, which made me curl my toes with pleasure. A few minutes later, I grabbed his head and pulled him up. 'Condom. Inside me, now.'

'Yes, ma.'

We fucked three times.

Later on that night, he gave me three hundred thousand naira. 'I am not paying you for sex. I just like your brutal honesty, and I can see you have a really bright future.'

Even though we never quite put it in words, for nearly two years, Yele was my Plan B whenever I needed money. It was either that or prostitution if I wanted to survive and keep writing.

~

Our first break-up came after Susan sold my second book. I started to be a little bit more comfortable financially. Yele, on the other hand, began to unravel like the layers of an angry onion. He would get moody if I was unavailable for his needs or not picking up his calls.

'Yele, I am editing. I have to revise the book with my editors.'

'Are you the first person to write a novel? Even that woman who is a popular feminist has a relationship. She is married!'

'You and I are not married.'

'Ara, I have been there for you. All I am asking is that you make time for me.'

'Okay.'

As the second book was close to publishing, the fights got bigger, and he became more abusive with his words.

'You need time to think. Call me when you return to your senses,' he said to me one afternoon before storming out.

I didn't call, and he eventually rang a month later.

'So, after our last fight, you didn't think you should apologise?'

'Good evening, Yele.'

'Ara, you are becoming proud.'

'No, I am just tired of you dictating when and how this – whatever we are doing – is going to go. We fight and you leave for a month?'

'To teach you a lesson.'

'You are not my father.'

'I am older than you. Respect the penis and its owner.'

'Okay.'

'Anyway, how have you been surviving? I know that your *yeye* publisher has not paid you.'

'I have some money from the last time we saw one another.'

'No wonder now. That's why you can afford to be doing anyhow. When we first met, if I didn't talk to you, within two weeks you would send me nudes. I need to start cutting down what I give you.'

I broke up with him after that call and changed my number.

The second book came out and I was doing readings in Lagos when he showed up with his daughter.

'I love your writing,' she squealed at me after the reading was done and I was signing books. 'I had to beg my dad to bring me. He is over there.' She pointed him out. He was watching his daughter and me with keen interest, but he kept his distance. His beard nearly covered his face.

'Oh. So, your father is not a fan?'

'He is! He is just shy.' She turned to him and beckoned. 'Daddy, come!'

He walked over and smiled at me. 'Hi. I am now a bigger fan after hearing you read and speak about your work. I am glad I met you today. My daughter never stops talking about you.'

I figured he didn't want his daughter to know we knew each other. 'Ah, I see, no wonder you didn't want to bring your daughter here,' I responded, playing along.

'Oh no, I just don't go out often, because—'

His daughter rolled her eyes. 'Daddy, please, she is not asking for one of your boring political speeches. Please, can you sign his copy too?' I took the copy he had with him, signed it, and put in my new number. I handed the book back to him. His eyes widened when he saw the note, and he tucked the book away as if to keep our secret safe. He called me two days later.

'I am sorry about what I said before. I will learn to respect you more now, baby. Please, forgive me.'

'You can take me to dinner, and I'll forgive you.'

'How is tomorrow night?'

We had dinner the next day. He showed up in a traditional maroon outfit. I wore a skirt so short that if you looked hard enough, you could see my kitty. I offset this with an oversized shirt. When he got out to open the door, he nearly tripped over.

'You look so sexy. Forgive me for being so blunt.'

'Thank you.'

We went to Slo Lagos. He apologised again. He told me what he had been up to while we were apart. As he spoke about memories of our good times and how he was there for me when I had no one, I felt myself growing wet.

'I am ready to go now.'

He looked surprised. 'Why? Did you not like the food?'

'It was delicious.'

'Let me get you home.'

Once we were outside the restaurant, walking to his car, I asked him, 'Are you able to come over so you can fuck me tonight?'

His eyes smiled. 'Oh. So, that's what you have been thinking about?'

'Yes.'

'No, I can't leave my kids, but we can work something out.'

We did it in the car. In the back seat, he turned me over, squeezing both cheeks as he pushed my skirt up. He undid his trousers and slid into me. He turned my face towards him and kissed me.

'I have been hard since I saw you in that skirt.'

'Fuck me hard, then.'

'Oh baby, I have missed you.'

We went at it for ten glorious minutes.

That was how we got back together. This time we were dating. He was no longer my sugar daddy.

~

After a few months, we started to have issues again. He wanted me to devote more time to the relationship, and I had begun writing my third book. To avoid fighting, I sent him a text asking for space, then went silent on him. I didn't have the bandwidth for his tantrums. More importantly, I was having a mental block with one of my characters.

After many days of no writing, I decided to take a walk to see if I could find her among the strangers on the street. I walked from Jakande to Agungi, looking at faces, and watching people interact with each other and their environment. Three hours later, with sweat pouring down my face, I gave up. I went home and ran a cold shower.

'Hello, Ara. Why have you not been picking up my calls?' Yele was standing at the entrance of the bathroom.

'*Ye!*' I turned and nearly blacked out in shock.

He caught me before I slipped onto the bathroom floor.

The conversation after he carried me out of the shower was short. 'I am sorry. I didn't know what else to do. I didn't mean to scare you.'

'So, you broke into my house? How did you get a copy of my key?'

'I took the spare you have in the kitchen.'

'Without my knowledge?'

'Babe, we are dating. I should have a key to your house. Please, don't be upset.'

I wasn't sure how to feel that he had broken into my apartment. No one had ever gone to such an extent to get my attention.

So, once more, I took him back.

~

Yele suggested that I move to House Twenty-One Estate after my third book was announced. The news had gone viral, with many local readers asking to know where I lived so they could meet some of these characters that I had said I'd grown up with. I was also seeing odd pictures of me popping up on social media, which must have been taken by strangers. One person on Instagram tagged me in a post where I was ahead of her in a supermarket queue.

The post read, 'Is that the author of *Bodies Bodies Bodies*?' In the picture, I looked unkempt.

I shared my increasing agitation at these intrusions with Yele.

'Ara, move to Ikoyi. No one will harass you there. You are now a big author!'

'I can't afford Ikoyi.'

'Not yet,' he countered. 'But you will. I will pay for the first year and then you can sort the rest out.'

'No, it's fine. I don't need you to pay my rent anymore.'

'*Ehen*, you no longer need my money?'

'It's not like that. Truth is, I can afford Ikoyi, but I prefer to live below my means.'

'This your Miss Independence act is no good, let me pay.'

'I can afford to take care of myself now, why should I still be relying on you? You can buy me gifts instead.'

He laughed. 'Or you know what, I'll find something for you that will be affordable in Ikoyi.'

Things were going really well then.

One evening, I was idly scrolling through Twitter when I saw an article that caught my attention. It was written by a journalist who is notorious for outing influential figures who have skeletons in their closets. His exposés were damaging, if not career ending. This particular article was about politicians and their practice of keeping their families abroad because they felt Nigeria was not good enough for them. Yet they kept stealing from the country to fend for the family members.

The tweets under the article cited many politicians who did this, and I saw Yele's name among them. One user responded, saying that Yele had his three kids and wife abroad under the guise that they were separated.

But Yele told me he was divorced.

I took a screenshot and then looked up Yele Onechance's wife. Several images popped up, but the one that stuck out was taken a year earlier with Yele, his wife and their children smiling comfortably for the camera.

Divorced people don't look that comfortable.

So, I sent it to him with a text:

> Are you divorced or separated? Twitter says you are still married.

An hour later, he responded:

> What's the difference? My wife and I are no longer living under the same roof.

His response left me speechless.

I had plans to end things with him for good after I got back from my reading in Zimbabwe, but I came back from that trip already broken and didn't have the energy to break anything else around me.

THIRTY-THREE

More

THURSDAY

12.45 p.m.

After leaving Juicy, I parked in a street close to the station. I brought out the food meant for her and started wolfing it down. I was halfway through the meal when an email notification came through on my phone.

Dear Ara,

Is that girl Juicy, whose case you asked me to look into, not the one who killed her sugar daddy? I don't think my law firm can take on her case. If you were asking me to help the wife, we could consider it, because it would be good publicity for the firm.

Anyway, if you say you want me to look into it, I can. I'll ask one of the legal assistants to get onto it. Since Juicy is your neighbour, please send me anything you have on her. We can discuss the cost later if I decide to represent her.

By the way, I flew through your second and third books. Wow. Would you please sign them when we meet?

Best wishes,

Ezu

I finished the last piece of my chicken wrap and headed home.

~

I'm not sure what one is meant to wear when meeting a neighbour at eleven p.m. But before I left Juicy, she asked me to go to House Seventeen at this time. I choose the long-sleeved ankara gown I wore to one of my readings in Ghana. It is tied at the waist with a flimsy belt that will come undone easily with a tug. I walk outside and am grateful I chose this light gown because the warm air that hits me is stifling. I head towards House Seventeen.

After several minutes, I arrive, knock and wait. No one answers, nor do I hear the sound of footsteps. I knock again.

'Who is it?' A voice speaks through the intercom. It's oddly familiar.

'My name is Ara. I am your neighbour.'

'How can I help you?'

Do I say *ashewo* into the intercom? What if my neighbour is not alone? Perhaps she is with her own sugar daddy.

'Yes?' the voice persists.

Wait, isn't that Rude Victoria?

I lean into the bell and whisper, 'Juicy says *ashewo*.'

'Excuse me?!'

'Juicy says *ashewo*!'

'Aunty, stop shouting. I am coming.'

The speaker clicks off, and a minute later, I hear rushed footsteps coming towards me. The door opens, and Rude Victoria grits her teeth, blocking the entrance with her body.

'What do you want?'

'I want to rent a secret.'

'Why?!'

'She wants to know what happened that night.'

She looks at me as if she wishes I would drop dead. 'Juicy is just a bitch, really. Come in!'

She turns and walks into the house, and I follow reluctantly. What business could Juicy have with Rude Victoria? The floor is lined with silver tiles. I see our images reflected in them. Victoria is already dropping her robe.

'Please don't waste my time, writer!'

I take my dress off too. I can't help but stare at her mottled skin, which has many different hues as if the creator was experimenting with her to see what shade suited her best.

She is looking at my small breasts and belly. I take the

opportunity to look at her further. Her breasts are humble yet stand proud and pert, showing no signs of sagging. I don't dare look further down.

'Okay, hurry and go to the backyard.' She points towards the door, and we dress in silence. As I step outside, I see her yard is empty, unlike most of the others, with no furniture at all. She follows and comes to stand in front of me, examining my face.

'You really need to wear some make-up.'

I almost choke. This woman whose foundation doesn't match her natural skin tone is telling me to start wearing make-up? I smile as I respond, 'I am afraid I don't know my foundation match. And I don't want to look like a clown.' I hope she catches my insult. It appears to go straight over her head.

'You'll have to sit on the ground, as I'm getting my furniture reupholstered. My children have ruined it with their crayons,' she says.

'I'll stand, thank you.'

'What's your secret?!'

I step closer to her, though making sure we are not touching.

'I had a boyfriend, and I was thinking of killing him too, before Juicy's news came out.'

'Your turn.'

She moves to whisper in my right ear. 'See, I was right

about you. You are like those hungry bloggers.' She leans back to see if she has sparked a reaction. I smile once more.

'Your secret?' I repeat.

'Juicy is my cousin.'

I feel the ground shift slightly, and she is looking into my eyes. 'You should sit down,' she suggests. I collapse to the floor. The cold tiles contrast against the warmth of my legs, jolting me back into the present.

This is going to be a long night.

'I presume you are writing a book about Juicy. And I have had time to look you up. Three-time international bestseller, huh? Impressive!' She sits down close to me. 'I want you to pay my full rent before I tell you Juicy's secret.'

Perhaps I was wrong. This may be a short night, and I can just fill in the details for my book from my imagination. I write fiction, after all, not real life.

I get up to leave. 'I am not writing a book, I am just here as Juicy's—'

'I know who killed Njoku and I will tell you.'

This bitch.

'Really?' I turn to her, wearing what I hope is a calm expression. 'Your neighbours seem to believe they know who did too.'

Her eyes narrow. 'Which neighbours?'

'We have traded too many secrets tonight. Besides, why would you want your cousin to rot in jail?'

She starts to laugh in an ugly way. Without missing a beat, I mimic her. Surprise slowly spreads across her face.

Ahn ahn, aunty, you thought you could be the only insane person in the room. Okay.

'I don't care what happens to Juicy. But fine. Pay me two hundred thousand naira!' she says to me.

'A hundred thousand,' I counter. I can see her making a calculation. I'll wait it out. I am prepared to remain in this house until a good number of my questions are answered.

She hisses, 'It's because you know I need the money.'

Yes, dear. I do.

'I will pay for your Netflix subscription for three months.'

'One hundred thousand naira and six months of Netflix,' she counters.

This woman is not well.

I sit back down, in the same position as before.

'For the Netflix subscription, I want the story about why you hate your cousin so much.'

She smiles.

'Oh, I'll tell you that for free.'

I was right. It *is* going to be a long night.

'Juicy is actually a bitch. How hard is it to sit in jail for a few months? We would get her out after. This is why I can't stand her. Always thinking of herself first. I didn't even know we were cousins till I ran into her at a party. I had heard of her. The fine girl with edges who had all the big men running to the University of Lagos to see her. So, when I saw her at a party, I walked up to her, and we started talking. She was really nice, which I found very annoying, but I didn't show it. I wanted her to like me, so I stayed talking to her for a long time. Turns out her father and mine are brothers, which was shocking because in all of the times I saw my father, he never mentioned having a sibling. But then I only saw my father once a year.

'Anyway, we decided to stick together. But Juicy was already a big girl, and I had a son. I expected her to be a little more giving. All that money and all those men – why not share with your new family? No o. Aunty would send me thirty thousand naira every weekend. For what, please? What is that supposed to buy in this city?'

'I am confused. When did you meet her?'

'Four years ago. She was doing her diploma.'

'She was only eighteen,' I say out loud before I can help myself.

'And so?! She was already driving a Range Rover. If you can drive Range at eighteen, be ready for problem.'

'Hmmm.'

'This is Nigeria. How many people make a living off being hardworking? So please keep your lectures to yourself. I had a first degree, a master's degree, and a child. The best jobs I could get only paid eighty thousand naira and I was living at Mowe – you know that town on the outskirts of Lagos state?'

I stare at her without acknowledging the question, hoping she continues.

She rolls her eyes. 'Anyway, after a few handouts from Juicy, I decided to take out a loan to *tush* myself up and get a proper sugar daddy. My first was the boss of the bank where I worked as a customer service representative. He moved me from Mowe to Ikeja.'

She stops to take a deep breath. 'When I moved to Ikeja with my son, Juicy and I started to move in similar circles. She tried to be nice and claim family, but she was competition, and soon after I fell pregnant again by my sugar daddy, so I didn't have space for family love. The sugar daddy left the country without even letting me know. I found out online and when I tried to tell him I was pregnant, he blocked me.'

She stops to look at me. 'Eventually I met a man who was separated from his wife, and he moved me here. Life was good until he dumped me. Two years later, Juicy came here too. And she was with the same man who had dumped me.'

I ask quietly, 'So why did you pretend not to know her that day when the news broke?'

'Because I don't. She is not my child. I only know my children.'

I am speechless.

She smiles at me. 'So, the secret you paid for? Are you ready? Many people killed Njoku. Juicy was framed.'

'You said before that it was one person.'

'I lied.'

'So, who are they?'

'*Ahn ahn*, Writer, that is not how it works. You want more, you pay more.'

My throat becomes tight as if Rude Victoria is choking me with invisible hands.

'Thank you for your time.' I get up to leave and she quickly adds:

'Ms Writer, we have all agreed to tell the agent we would consent to a two hundred thousand maximum increase on the rent. Just letting you know in case you speak with him, as we women have to stick together.' She clasps her hands together and raises them to support her words.

This woman is still worried about the rent?! And talking about women sticking together when Juicy is still in jail?

I walk as fast as I can out of her house, then break into a run.

THIRTY-FOUR

Self-Care

FRIDAY

10 a.m.

Juicy says I may need therapy, and I think she might be right. The morning I heed her advice, I decide to use an Uber, so I don't have to deal with insane Lagos drivers on my way to see the therapist I booked. As expected, the driver calls once he sees the destination.

'Good morning, madam, this is Mr Uyo. I just want to be sure, are you going to Yaba Left? The hospital? The psychiatric hospital?' The high pitch in his voice is battling with the unstable phone network.

'Good morning, sir. Yes, I am,' I respond.

'Who is the mad person? You or the person you are going to visit?'

'No one is mad, sir.'

'That's not the question I asked you, Ma. I can't go if I

don't know who is mad in the situation. Are you the mad person, is the person you are going to visit the mad person, and if they are, are you also bringing them back and expecting me to drive you?'

'I am a student going for research purposes, sir, and I will book another Uber once I am done.'

He sighs. 'Okay. That's all I wanted to confirm. I am on my way, Ma.'

As we drive into the compound of the hospital, orderlies in white overalls are dragging a man and woman in, who I soon find out were cheating on their partners with each other. The man had left his bride-to-be for the woman, who was their wedding planner. Allegedly, one of the jilted partners had placed a curse on them.

'So, what now happened? Did they run mad?' I ask the nurse who was kind enough to share the story with me as I fill out the form.

She starts to laugh. 'Aunty, if they didn't run mad, how did they end up here?'

'This is serious.'

The nurse laughs again. 'Who did you bring, Aunty? Are they in the car? Let me help find hospital assistants that will bring them in.'

I take a deep breath and answer, 'I brought myself. I have come to treat my own issues.' She takes several steps back, chanting, 'Blood of Jesus. I have been talking to a mad person.'

I attempt to touch her, and she screams, 'Don't touch me!' Her cries attract another nurse, who joins us, asking, 'Is everything okay? What's the problem?'

The first nurse points at me. 'She—'

I cut in, 'No, please, I am not mad. I just have some issues.'

Both nurses look at each other, so I lean in, and the first nurse speaks rather sternly to me. 'Aunty, please take a step back. We are not allowed to be this close to patients.'

I smile, hoping to calm her down. 'I am not a patient. I am just looking for a therapist.'

'In Yaba Left? What happened to the internet?'

I move closer. 'Go back! Don't make me tell them to come and tie you up,' she warns. The second nurse leans on the counter, watching as the drama between her colleague and I unfolds. I step back again. 'Ma, I am not mad, I just have some issues I think speaking with a therapist will help me understand.'

A lanky, unkempt figure appears out of nowhere in a white lab coat, and the nurse speaking to me snaps her bony fingers at him. 'Doctor Rogba, all the other doctors are on ward round. Do you have space to see another patient today?'

The man smiles. 'Is it an emergency?'

She points at me. 'She is the patient. Does she look like an emergency?'

The doctor comes to stand beside me. 'Mrs Ishola, your rudeness never fails to astound me. I don't have time today. Have you taken her vitals and asked all the necessary questions?'

'Not yet. I didn't know she was the patient. We were talking—'

'Send her to me in another five hours. I have a home emergency that just came up. A popular musician,' he adds as he walks away.

I turn to the nurses with a smile.

'I can't wait for the next five hours. Can I reschedule for another day?'

The first nurse clasps her hands behind her head. 'My sister, let me just advise you. We have a backlog of patients. Many people are now on codeine and loud, so the hospital is fuller. If you are not mad, Yaba Psychiatric is not for you. Go online to book a therapist.'

'I don't want an online therapist, I want to see whoever is available to share my story with in person. And I don't know where else to get therapy here in Lagos that is affordable.'

'Then go to church. Talk to a pastor. They will refer you to a guidance counsellor!'

'I am not sure I can trust a pastor with my secrets.'

'Then your case is worse. What you need is deliverance, Ma, not therapy!' the nurse responds. The other one chuckles and walks away from the scene.

'Please,' I start to plead with her.

She cuts in, 'Ma, we have people who have been in wards for months, with no doctor to treat them. You know that most medical practitioners in Nigeria are either on their way out of the country or with private clinics. You are not a priority case. You will not be treated, nor would a therapist be assigned to you in the next two months.' She steps away from the counter to look at me. 'You are not wearing torn clothing or walking barefoot. My sister, your case is not that bad. We all have issues, we are still here! Let me give you the number of my pastor.' She scribbles something on a piece of paper. 'Take this and go, my pastor can help you within two days. And your problems will disappear.'

I take the paper. 'Thank you.'

Perhaps after this book is out, I will revisit therapy again.

~

I decide to go and see Juicy's mother and aunty to make this wasted day more fruitful. I didn't call ahead and plan to catch them by surprise. If they are not available, then I can leave a message or give them a call.

The Uber driver – a slender fellow in a lilac T-shirt and a cap – tunes to a radio station broadcasting inspirational messages as we drive to Ajegunle. He doesn't seem bothered that he is picking me up from a psychiatric hospital. After ten minutes, he speaks. His baritone voice, which takes me by surprise given his slight appearance, booms through the vehicle.

'Madam. Why not take the trip off the app?'

I look at my phone. 'But they are already charging me.'

'It's due in cash. If I end the trip on the app, I don't have to take the money from you.'

'Okay. I will pay you twenty thousand for each leg of the trip.'

'Madam, no. Fuel cost is high. Pay fifty thousand to Ajegunle and the same to Badagry.'

I check the app to compare the fare to both places as we go past a dingy motel. It's a fair bargain but I don't want to give in too easily.

'Let's do twenty-five thousand naira for each.'

'Okay.'

He turns up the volume on the radio, and the voice of a pastor who just bought a private jet with all the offerings and contributions from his followers, accompanies us as we drive.

~

Raw. Mayhem.

Those are the two words that adequately describe Ajegunle. The tall buildings are densely packed together, with only a tiny space between them for passers-by. The noise from the streets outside almost drowns out the preacher's voice streaming from the radio inside the car. Everyone is either talking to someone or going somewhere. Children run in between the cars that have slowed to a crawl because the streets are so narrow.

'Where are you going, Madam?'

I fish the address out. 'Number 3, Idi Street.'

'My map doesn't work here. We have to use our eyes and street sense.'

We find a place to park close to a carpenter's workshop. The minute we step out of the car, a thick-set man with a protruding belly in off-white overalls comes out of nowhere and points a log of wood at us.

'Carry your car.'

The driver walks over to him. 'Good afternoon, sir. We are going to number 3—'

'Carry your car. They will steal your mirror and engine in thirty minutes, and you won't know.'

I move close to them, standing beside the driver. 'We will leave now, *Baba*. We just need directions, please.'

He swallows and his chins wobble. 'The next street is Idi. The house *wey* you *dey* go is on your left. Carry your car.'

'But *Baba*, these roads are so tight.'

'I will wait here with the car, sir, and we can chop pepper soup and beer together while madam goes,' the driver says.

He looks at us and then stares at me. '*Sisi*, where is your husband?'

'I am still looking for one.'

'Big woman like suppose get husband. A man that will follow you everywhere. This Ajegunle, you need a man to follow you around. You can't be walking by yourself.'

In that case, a bodyguard would be much better than a husband, I think, but I hold my tongue and smile.

'Driver,' he instructs. 'Go with her. Your car is safe. Drop ten thousand naira.'

The driver looks like he's getting ready to negotiate the price. I speak over him.

'Okay, *Baba*. We will give it to you when we come back.'

'Okay. Be going now.'

We follow his instructions, walking the narrow street where people and piles of rubbish are competing for space. At the address, I see a young girl in a blue spaghetti strap vest and knickers, fetching water at the entrance of the two-storey duplex.

I signal to the driver to wait as I walk towards her. Once she turns the tap off, I ask:

'*Sisi*, I am looking for Juicy's mother. My name is—'

'She *dey* back. Walk through to the back of the house. She is cooking.'

'Oh, can I just go—'

'Yes, follow from here to the back and you will see a small shed. She is cooking there.'

I make my way down a muddy thoroughfare to where

a woman is bent over, balancing a pot on the pulsing blue flames of a locally made stove. I look around and see no one else. This must be her.

As if sensing my presence, she stands up straight, and turns to look at me. She looks nothing like Juicy, except for the same thick eyebrows.

'Good afternoon, aunty, who are you looking for?'

'Are you Juicy's mother?'

Her expression remains unchanged. 'Yes, who are you? I hope you are not another press person.'

'No, I am her neighbour.'

'Is that so? What do you want?'

'I wanted to ask a few questions.'

'Is she owing rent?'

'No, ma.'

'Is she owing you?'

'No, ma.'

'And you are not press?'

'No, ma.'

'Then please, I want nothing to do with a child that has disgraced the family, and if you know what's good for you, you will leave this place before I pour hot water on you.'

Her eyes tell me she means every word.

God forbid I let anyone strip me of my epidermis.

'Sorry to disturb you, ma.'

I beat a hasty retreat back along the same path and find the driver leaning against a bald palm tree.

'Let us go.'

He pulls away from the trunk of the tree and walks to the car as I open the passenger door. The pot-bellied car-defender is nowhere to be found.

'Where in Badagry are we going, madam?' he asks as he starts the car.

I check the address. 'A place called Awhanjigo.'

'Oh, I know that place. What's the number of the house?'

'Number 87.'

~

Two hours later, we arrive at our destination. Awhanjigo looks like an abandoned village, with whitewashed box-like buildings stacked close to each other. There are people by the roadside selling brooms and Rafia mats. This time, the house is easy to find because numbers are boldly written on the sides of the buildings in black paint.

We park close by. The driver turns the car off and turns to me. 'This place no get trouble like Ajegunle.'

'Yes, I know.'

'Do you need me to follow you, madam?'

I don't know what to expect from Juicy's aunt, so I say, 'Yes, please.'

Together, we exit the car and walk up to the brown gate and knock three times. A voice immediately responds.

'Yes?'

'Good afternoon. Please, I am looking for Mrs Nwaduka.'

'From where?'

'I'm here on behalf of Juicy.'

'Juicy *wey dey* police station?'

'Yes.'

'The person you *dey* find no *dey*.'

'Please—'

'Mrs Nwaduka is not around, Aunty! She has travelled to the village. She will not come back for six months.'

I turn and walk back to the car. If this is what family looks like, I am glad to be an orphan. Knowledge is not always power, sometimes it just breaks the heart.

I should not have bothered going anywhere today.

THIRTY-FIVE

More Wahala

MONDAY

9.58 a.m.

The station is empty except for two officers – including the one I met the first day I came – and a handcuffed, young-looking offender with tribal marks across his face, who is wearing only plaid boxers.

The female officer sees me as soon as I step inside.

'*Ahn*, madam, come with me. It is you we are waiting for, please finish early today. We have a naming ceremony.'

'Okay. Good morning.' I pick up my pace to keep up with her as she limps excitedly to the usual venue.

'I have gotten you a lawyer,' I say to Juicy once the officer leaves.

She puts a hand to her hair and looks puzzled. 'I have a lawyer.'

'No. You have someone who I don't believe even finished

law school. I got you someone better than your current representative.'

'I don't have money—'

'I know. We will sort something out,' I respond, fiddling with the strap of my Winston leather bag.

Her eyes nearly fling me against the mouldy walls.

'Are you a pimp? Because I don't believe you can be living off writing alone. Are you helping me so that you can become my pimp when I get out?'

'I am not a pimp. I am just helping you.'

'With money from where?'

'From my work. I make a decent living as a writer. It wasn't always the case, but I'm doing good now. My third book is also making a lot of waves, so my royalties are better. The point is writing takes really good care of me . . . ' I pause my rant and continue to fiddle with the strap.

'I don't know why I get snappy with you, Ara. I am sorry.' She smiles at me. 'Okay. I'll accept your help. Thank you.'

'You are welcome.'

'You didn't come yesterday.'

'I went to look for a therapist.'

She comes to sit next to me. 'How did it go?'

'Not good.'

'Awww. I am sorry.'

'It's okay. It's not your fault. Um, I also went to see your family members.'

Her eyes dim, her lips twitching as she forces a smile. 'I already know it went badly. Like I told you.'

'You were right. I'm sorry.'

She fixes her beautiful, clear eyes on my face. 'Thank you for trying. I am sorry about therapy. I guess I also won't be trying it.' She draws me into a hug and I bury my face in her shoulder, inhaling the smell of soap and baby oil as she relaxes into me. A few minutes later, we let each other go, and she sits on the chair across from me.

'Today, I want to talk to you about what I wanted for my life.'

I bring out the recorder and place it on the table.

PLOT TWIST

THIRTY-SIX

Juicy's Confession V

I lost a baby when I turned sixteen.

The father of the baby I lost was called Kindness. Like every time I remember that I slept with a guy called Kindness, I laugh at how love is such a scam it makes us blind to everything, even names. Anyway, his unusual name made him popular among the other students. We sat beside each other in class for three years, but we never spoke. Everyone knew I preferred the company of older, richer men. I started the whole sugar baby business when I turned fifteen – my mother said men like women young. Anyway, Kindness finally spoke to me when we got to our final year of secondary school and were paired on a chemistry project. We eventually became friends, and he kept asking why I liked to follow big men. I told him the truth. I was my family's main breadwinner, and I had to take care of my parents. He advised me to focus on our final year exams since I had always been a strong student, suggesting I could apply for a scholarship and maybe go abroad.

Honestly, I thought he was just trying to get into my pants by being nice to me, but that was not the case. I tried to seduce him many times while we were working on our project together. He always refused. Like he insisted that he wanted me to be a better person. He offered to give me money, not a lot, but it was enough to keep my parents satisfied.

Kindness was the first reason I stopped being a sugar baby. You already know about the second time. With his help, I was still able to take care of my family while focusing on school. I passed my final certificate examinations in one sitting and was very happy. We started dating after we graduated, and somehow, I ended up pregnant. But he was not upset. We had a plan. We would go to Canada, enrol in college, and then grow our family as we worked.

The mistake I made was telling my mother I was pregnant, and that Kindness was my boyfriend. She drugged my food that night. When I woke up, I had bled heavily, and the baby was gone. I will never forget her words.

'This family is suffering, and you want to follow man for love. You are not serious. This your beauty will be used properly.'

When he came around the next day, my mother told Kindness I had gone away. I was in the house, but I was too weak to fight her. After she came back inside, she told me boys like that don't marry girls like me.

She was right. Look at me now. Not married. Not chosen. Abandoned in a prison cell.

THIRTY-SEVEN

Bombshells

MONDAY
12.34 p.m.

As I exit the station, a motorcyclist carrying two passengers like a human sandwich nearly collides with the back of my car. He stops to jab a finger at me. 'Madam, *dey* look where you *dey* go! If you are tired of life, get to your house first and die there.'

'You are a madman!' I yell as he zooms off, before parking to check if he did any damage to my car. My phone rings. 'This is not a good time, Dotun,' I say as soon as I pick up. Once I'm satisfied that the car is not dented, I walk back to the driver's side.

She sighs. 'Ara, you can be so rude. What happened to hello?'

'Hello, Dotun, this is not a good time.'

I get into the driver's seat, checking the map for a less busy route.

'We have received an offer for the film and TV rights for your three books,' Dotun continues. 'I have forwarded the contract to you. It's so good, we are taking it. They want to go into pre-production for the first book next year. Erm, sweetheart, can you please write a short story for *Pole* magazine in the meantime? The one that listed you under their writers to watch last year? They are focusing on women this month and they reached out to see if you would like to contribute a piece for them. Just two thousand words?'

I clench my fists to stop the heat slowly rising in me. 'Dotun, no. I can't fucking write a short story right now. Did you forget that I am on a deadline? You want me to abandon the book for a story?! Look, I will review the film rights offer, but if you say it's good, then it's good. We will take it. But I am not writing a fucking piece!'

'Ha. Sooo dramatic this one. Okay o.'

I take a deep breath before saying, 'I have to go.'

Another motorcyclist pulls up by my car and yells, 'Move away your car, my friend. Is it because you are driving a big car?!'

I am tempted to chase him and run him over.

~

I resume writing once I get home. Three thousand words in, the characters begin to play games with me, so I take a break to restructure the fictional world of the characters again while lying in bed. I jot ideas on my notepad while I also check my phone, hoping for a call from Ezu. In his last email, he said they may be able to get Juicy out on bail. Njoku's wife's current lawyer owes him a favour. With any luck, the bail is likely to be set at one million naira.

I hear my phone ring. Dotun again!

I really need to block this woman.

'Hello, Dotun, I have told you, I am not writing a story. Please, you can't convince me.'

'*Na wa*, you this girl. I am not calling about that—'

'Okay, so why are you—'

Rinnngggg.

My doorbell cuts me off. *Who could it be at this time?*

'—a TED Talk in Houston in January.'

Huh?

'TED Talk? Me? Which January?'

I am walking to the door as the doorbell continues to saw through the air with noise.

'The one that is staring at us, dear,' Dotun says. 'And you can't say no, Ara. You are now a Women's Prize for Fiction-nominated writer. You need to show up at events and talk about yourself more.'

'Dotun, please hold on.' I am now downstairs and standing before the door. I swap the phone to my left ear and peep out with my right eye. I almost drop the phone.

'Helloooo. Ara, can you hear me?'

I grip the phone harder as I say, 'Fine. Ted Talk. January. Got it. I have to call you back.'

'No. Don't even dare cut the call on me again—'

I set the phone down for a moment by the chrome vase of flowers, putting Dotun on speaker. I tighten my robe as she rambles on.

'Ara, we are working on your visa so send the damn passport you say has been with immigration for nearly a year. Get your shit together and submit your book. You won't have time to write next year—'

I end the call and turn to open the door.

Njoku's wife, Edith, walks into my house, followed by all the women in the estate, the side-chicks of her late husband, in single file.

~

They sit on the L-shaped sofa and I perch on the armchair across from them. It is only now, looking at them together, that I work out the source of the nagging familiarity I felt looking at some of them. They all look like a version of Juicy. I recognise a tired Juicy, slightly darker-skinned Juicy, older Juicys, and Juicys of different sizes. Perhaps it is the other way around, and Juicy is the younger, fresher version of these women.

I would give anything to ask Njoku – the silent, dead elephant in the room – how he chose his women. Are there also women in this estate who look like me and have dated Yele? Am I also part of an unholy cult?

What is this life?

They have only been here for a few minutes, but I am starting to feel feverish. My phone rings once more.

'Pick up the call,' my neighbour who has both male and female parts says. I obey.

'Ara, how far?' Ezu's voice travels through the receiver.

'Ezu, please can you text me?'

'Ah. Okay, but we can't get the girl bail. That man's wife is—'

'—Text me.'

I cut him off and put down the phone.

Njoku's wife smiles at me.

Yes, this is the one that looks the most like Juicy. The Juicy prototype.

She leans forward. 'Hi, Bawarin. We don't know each other. My name is Edith. I am Njoku's wife.' Her gentle voice should have diffused the tension in the room but it does the opposite.

Did she just call me Bawarin?

'Hello,' I respond.

She crosses her legs, revealing smooth skin beneath her sequin dress.

Isn't this the woman that looked so sick in court one week ago?

She smiles. 'I'll cut to the chase, Ms Writer. I hear you have been asking questions and collecting stories.'

'I have.'

'You can't write this story.'

'Why not?' I blurt out.

Shit.

She looks around at the other women. 'I told you people she was writing! How could you have believed a writer wouldn't write? Especially someone like her, whose books have been so popular, controversial and successful!'

My eyes dart across their faces. Some of the women look at me with stormy expressions, and the others just stare at the floor. Edith addresses me again.

'Bawarin, dear, if you write this story, you will have to include the part where you tell us how you gave your son up for adoption.'

My heart sinks. Her smile deepens, revealing the faintest of dimples.

'I know a lot about you, Ara. I read up on you on the internet. But to know more about Bawarin, I had to speak to your house mother in Ogbomosho. She told me everything. She said to tell you she is proud of how far you have come.'

'I—'

'My darling, *biko* don't say anything, just drop the story, let Juicy rot in jail and your secret will be safe. How do you think the international community will feel knowing you lead a double life, that you are a mother who abandoned her own child? *Oyinbo* people don't like scandal o—'

'Listen, Ara,' someone else says. I turn to look. It's Burqa. 'We don't want to end your career. Women support women in this estate. But this Juicy matter—'

Edith cuts her off. 'Kill it. Kill the story and write something else.'

'What happens if I don't?' I whisper.

They all start to laugh, and then as if they are summoned by a clarion call, they get up and file out in a single straight line.

THIRTY-EIGHT

Deleayo

MONDAY
10.38 p.m.

Every time I remember my pregnancy, I like to borrow the verb *fell* that a famous Nigerian blogger used when she announced her pregnancy.

I *fell pregnant* at sixteen.

His name was Vincent. We came to the orphanage at the same time. We were ten years old. I arrived in the morning, and he came in the evening on the same day. We stood out as the children who, year after year, did not find a home. Even though we never spoke to each other, often when our eyes met, he would smile at me. I always left books out for him, though I don't think he read much because he was forever failing English classes.

Six years in, he approached me one evening in the playground and said, 'You are my girlfriend.'

I just shrugged. 'Okay.'

Because of the watchful eyes of the house mother, being his girlfriend didn't change much for me except that he stopped eating some of his meals and gave them to me, and I in turn wrote his assignments for him. We couldn't speak often. But we wrote letters to each other and then tore them up so we wouldn't be caught.

I never told him about my desire to meet my parents, because the orphanage had hardened most of us who had not been adopted, and any sign of weakness was mocked.

One afternoon, while everyone else was out in the playground, he came over to my desk, where I was reading.

'Bawa, come with me.' I stood up and followed him. We got to the toilet. He started to unbuckle his trousers, and I was waiting, watching him struggle with the belt. He stopped and said to me, 'Lift up your skirt.'

'Why?'

'I want to show you something. Don't worry, you will like it.'

I lifted the pleated skirt. He took his finger and started fiddling with my underwear and rubbing himself. His eyes rolled to the back of his head.

'Is everything okay? What are you doing?'

He ignored me and kept rubbing. Then he stopped suddenly and rested his head against the tiled wall of the toilet. After a few minutes, he smiled at me. 'Did you like it?'

'No. Everywhere is hot.'

'Don't worry, you will,' he said. 'Now drop your skirt and let's go.'

Eventually, we progressed to exploring each other's bodies. Then, one afternoon when the house mother was away on a family trip and other volunteers were with the younger children, Vincent and I had sex. It was painful at first. The bloodstains left on the blue *aso oke* we laid on scared me. But Vincent said it would get better, and it did. I looked forward to our meetings because it made life at the orphanage bearable. My daily routine became waking up, attending classes, reading books, meeting up with Vincent, and sleeping.

Months into our relationship, my boobs started to get bigger and feel sore. My tongue would swell up in the morning and I began to feel very sluggish. I told Vincent about the changes in my body. He explained I was going through the process of becoming a woman.

'Becoming a woman means my tongue should swell up?'

'It's because you are special,' he teased me.

One hot morning, the house mother looked at me casually and asked, 'Bawa, *ta ló fún e· lóyún?*'

'Ma?'

'Who owns the bastard inside your belly?!'

'Nobody. I ate too much *akamu* this morning, that's why my stomach is big,' I replied, fidgeting. Out of nowhere, a blow landed on my left cheek. She kept slapping me until I confessed to her what Vincent and I had been doing.

'You are a senseless girl. You that don't have a father and mother, you have now gone to carry *pikin*. If you are hungry for man, don't you have the sense to use a condom?'

'I am not pregnant, ma. I am just becoming a woman.'

She dragged me to the clinic in the orphanage and the nurse asked me to pee on a stick. I remember staying in the toilet for a long time, wishing it were a dream. The house mother came over and forced me out. I handed the test stick to the nurse, who let out a sigh and said:

'Pregnant.'

The house mother slammed something on my head, and I blacked out.

When I regained consciousness, I found myself in a bed, surrounded by the house mother and several volunteers. She leaned in and said, 'You will bring this child into the world because I believe in doing what's right. There's someone who wants to adopt a new baby, and they will take the child to London. You are very lucky. This baby won't end up like you.'

That was it. I was locked away in another room for the remainder of my pregnancy. I wasn't allowed to play with other children or come out when we had visitors. I couldn't go to school, and everything became about the baby. Slowly, I started to hate the child, and I wanted it out of me so I could get back to my life.

One day, water started running down my legs, and the knife-like pain in my lower belly made me call out to the volunteers. I was taken to a private clinic, and nine hours later, he came into the world, screaming. After I gave birth, they asked me to name the baby. I called the child Deleayo, which was a prayer that the child would find a good home.

'Vincent can no longer stay here as we are required by law to report his conduct and protect the other children. We are taking care of children here, not raising babies delivered by them,' she told me once I returned to the girls' dormitory. 'However, because you are a woman, we have made plans for you to stay here so we can look after you.'

Vincent was moved to another orphanage, and I never saw him again.

By now, I had missed the window to sit my exams for admission into the University of Lagos. I was too old to be adopted and too young to live by myself as an adult. I didn't fit anywhere.

'Why don't you do something else for a year, you can teach the other children in the orphanage? We can't pay you, but you can continue to stay here. You never know, if you do well, you may become a volunteer. Then you can have all these nice, nice things,' the house mother suggested two months later.

I took her up on her offer and put all of my energy into teaching the children in the orphanage for two years.

During my free time, I read books and forgot about getting a formal university education since I was never given a chance nor earning enough to retake them. The house mother kept making excuses when I asked to take the entrance examination into the university. 'Bawa, you want me to give you the money for another child so you can write Gce? After you carry *belle.*'

'Read all those your books, you can learn from there now.'

'Bawa, I didn't go to school and I am a big woman, you don't need school.'

My life felt like being in a traffic jam, stalled and going nowhere anytime soon.

~

One Friday, me and the other volunteers had taken the younger children to the playground. The house mother had stopped accompanying us after a fall the year before, while trying to cut some bananas in the compound. The injury left her with a permanently bad leg, and she couldn't stand for long anymore. She began to spend most of the time when we were outside going through everyone's belongings and fishing out any contraband or food that we had hidden away from the kitchen that week. Most Fridays, we returned in fear because we knew she would have a nasty surprise waiting for us.

'*Ah ah*, stop right there!' She would burst out of her room.

'I found three fish bones under Onikan's bed. We only ate fish once this week and I gave all the children the head or middle part of the fish. These are tails. Where did they come from?!'

'Mummy, I am not the one who ate it,' Onikan, another one of the older children, would try to deny it.

'Shut up, *olè!* Go and pick-pin in that corner. Lift that one leg higher to the sky, it better not drop, or I will kill you! Bastard child!'

That Friday, as we got to the playground, I realised I had left my diary behind, and I wanted to write. So, I snuck off while the other children were playing hide and seek, headed to the girls' dormitory, gathered my writing things and was about to leave, when I heard the house mother singing to herself. As I tiptoed past, I bumped into a stack of buckets left in the corridor.

'*Ta nì ye·n?*' Her voice rang out immediately.

'It is me, Mummy,' I said with a muted voice.

'Bawarin?'

'Yes, ma.'

'Why are you not in the playground?'

'I forgot something, Mummy.'

'I hope you are not trying to steal food? If I measure out the rice in the cooler and any is missing, you know what will happen.'

'No, Mummy, I just came to pick up my diary.'

'You are still doing your foolish writing. Don't let me see you when I get out of the bathroom. Go now!' she screamed.

I walked away, afraid she would appear. Then I heard her mutter, 'Useless child.'

In that instant, something snapped in me. I walked back and knocked on her door.

'Yes?!' she bellowed, so loudly I thought the door might come off its hinges.

'One of the volunteers asked me to give you something, ma.'

'What?'

'A package, ma.'

'But you said you came to pick something up. Why are you a liar, Bawa? I'll deal with you later. Now just give me whatever it is!'

She opened the door with her arms stretched out, soap suds dripping from her face. She looked expectantly at me. I stood, frozen, unsure of what to do.

'*Ehn ehn*, where is the thing? Answer me, my friend. I have soap in my eyes.'

I pushed past her, into her room. She turned towards me. 'Bawarin, are you okay?'

Wham.

I caught her by surprise, smacking her hard across her face with my diary. Three times, in fact. She reeled back with the force of my blows, trying to rub the soap from her eyes. She was a foot taller than me, but I took advantage of her momentary blindness and slammed her against the wall. Then I dragged her over to the bed and pushed her back onto the mattress, grabbed her towel from the bed stand and stuffed the end into her mouth. I pulled a fresh cane from under her bed and got to work.

'*This* is for calling my mother a prostitute. *This* is for calling me a bastard. And *this* is for blaming me after my parents abandoned me! *This* is for all the nights you made us sleep outside! *This* is for taking away my joy.'

Whoosh. Whoosh. Whoosh.

I used the cane to trace a path down to her bad knee. She watched in horror as I hit it three times. Tears mingled with mucus as her muffled wails filled the room. I pressed the towel harder into her mouth and the cane came alive again.

Whoosh. Whoosh. Whoosh.

Then I stopped. Leaning over, I bent towards her.

'I am leaving this orphanage today.'

I went to the cupboard opposite her bed and took out the cooler of chicken she had fried that morning. I ransacked her bag, and the places where I knew she had been hiding cash donations over the years. I took all of it.

'Thank you for the chicken and the money, Monsura.' She gasped as I called her by her first name. I smiled.

That's right, you witch, I know your name and I can say it out loud.

Afterwards, I left her room and packed my things in a nylon bag. I travelled with the sun, walking down the unevenly tarmacked road, away from the orphanage, headed to Lagos.

~

Eight months ago, I received an invite to do a reading from my third book in Harare. The event took place at a disused but well-kept children's park. After the reading was done, I began to sign books, and a group of young women came over with their copies. One of them, who wore a pleated green skirt, black tank top and yellow bomber jacket, said to me, 'We love all your books, but especially the first one, *How to Murder your Parents.* It showed us how to be better parents. We are all teen mums, and we wanted to give up our children for adoption. Thanks to your book, we are keeping our children.'

I didn't know what to say to that, so I smiled and nodded.

'Do you have any advice for us? We are forming an organisation for girls who get pregnant in their teens.'

I wanted to say, *Don't get pregnant. Keep your legs closed.* Instead, I said, 'Don't let your mistakes define you.' They looked at me with tears in their eyes and hugged me.

It was the first time since I'd given Deleayo up for adoption that I realised what I had lost.

When I got back to Nigeria, all I could think about was my boy. I read articles about mothers who gave up their children for adoption and the ways they were able to find them, especially in Nigeria.

You can go back to the place of birth and ask the people around.

You can pray.

You can do juju and call the child's head home.

None of these suggestions was plausible, so I googled the orphanage. It was still running. They even had a website that listed all the children that had ever been through the home. I saw a blurry photo of myself at age fifteen with my old name. I searched for Vincent, but he wasn't listed. Then I typed my son's name into a search engine, but there was no Deleayo among the hundreds of names on the site.

What if Vincent had come back for his son?

Did they really take him to London?

What if I met my own child somewhere and didn't even know him?

He should be fourteen years old now. I have missed fourteen birthdays.

How could I just forget him for so long?

Was he even alive?

I sank deeper into despair.

But I couldn't spend eight months being depressed. I had a book to promote. I would wake up, wishing for Deleayo to run through the door and say, 'Good morning, Mummy,' or that he was beside me on the bed, greeting me before falling back to sleep. I carried these heavy feelings with me day after day like a cursed crown on my head.

I got through at least two physical book readings, an online interview, and a book club event every week for two months. But I couldn't bring myself to travel.

'My passport has expired and it's taking immigration a minute to renew it. You know how it is here,' became my excuse to decline invitations from outside Nigeria.

'I am currently unable to make it in person. I have family obligations. I am happy to do virtual book readings,' those were my excuses for events within the country.

Once I was done with whatever work obligations that I could muster the energy for, I would be on social media for hours on end, and, if it was during the weekend, I would fuck Yele. I didn't respond to any queries from my agent, but Dotun was harder to get rid of since we had a relationship outside of work.

After two months of forcing myself to carry on in this way, I stopped responding to any requests at all.

THIRTY-NINE

Another Manic Day

TUESDAY
7.30 a.m.

When my alarm wakes me up, I walk briskly into the shower, many thoughts running through my mind as I scrub. What do I do about Deleayo? What happens if the truth comes out? How can I tell Juicy's story without mentioning Deleayo?

After I shower, I slip into a denim jumpsuit, a pair of *ankara* sneakers and drape my blue Winston leather bag over my shoulder. I heat up some leftover pasta for Juicy before stepping out.

The stench hits my nose before I see it. A dead cat on my doorstep with the blood drained into a black bowl beside it.

I rush back inside.

My phone buzzes immediately. It is an email from Susan that I impulsively open with trembling hands.

Hi Ara,

Your US/UK editors are asking to see the first draft of the new book in another two weeks. Please just send whatever you have written.

Best,

Susan

I dial Mr Nicholas's number. It doesn't go through.

I dial Solomon's number. He picks up on the first ring.

FORTY

Clean-up

TUESDAY

8.45 a.m.

'Aunty Ara, I have cleaned it! You can come out now. No fear, ma.' Solomon's voice pulls me out of my trance on the sofa.

I step out, making sure to skirt around the wet spot. 'Thank you, Solomon.'

He says to me quietly, 'Aunty Ara, why you *dey chook* mouth for *wetin* no concern you? Person kill sugar daddy or she no kill sugar daddy. How is it your business, ma?' He stops to lean against the door and continues, '*Na* Madam Edith own half of this estate now since her husband *don* die. The only house that is not her own is Juicy's, that useless man gave Juicy that house. He will her the house. On top that, that man want remove Madam Edith for will. Imagine! His own wife!' he adds.

I clear my throat so the words can find a clear path. 'Solomon, what—'

'Aunty Ara, mind your business, ma.' He looks at me, a sinister smile forming on his face. 'And I really like you o. You be good tenant. You no get problem.'

My next words are slow and deliberate.

'Do you know anything about the murder?'

'I am the one that kill Mr Njoku. I enter the house when *e dey* sleep as he was waiting for Juicy and stab *am*. Then the women came, and chop *am* to pieces. We all plan to kill that useless woman beater and cheat. This *mata* big pass you. Juicy no deserve dis *wahala* but *na* life be that. Me, *na* Madam Edith cousin I be. She brought me from the village to work here. I am very valuable to her. I know all her secrets.'

'Did you put this cat here to scare me?'

He laughs. 'No, *na* this your next-door neighbour do that. Correct madwoman. Just try leave this Juicy *mata* alone, Aunty Ara. This country too corrupt for you to be fighting for justice for *ashewo*.'

I walk slowly to my car, stifling the urge to wail.

FORTY-ONE

The Call

TUESDAY

9.35 a.m.

Halfway through my journey, my phone rings.

'Ara, why are you going to the station to mess with police work?!' Yele screams once I pick up.

'Excuse me?'

'The DPO called me, he says you are disturbing them over that girl. The sugar daddy-killer.'

'Yele . . . '

He continues, his voice dropping a pitch lower, 'Baby, don't go and get mixed up in what you don't know about. Your career and everything you have worked so hard for is at stake.'

I sigh. 'So I've heard.'

'Why are you still going to see her?'

'Yele—'

'I know you don't talk about your work but if you are writing about her, I would advise you to stop.'

'Why?'

'Ara! What does book writing have to do with prostitution?'

I want to ask him how many of his mistresses live in the estate, but I really don't care.

'She is not a pros—'

'After tomorrow, don't go there again! I have told him to give you two more days at best.'

'Thank you.'

'That's okay. You know I love you.'

'Yele. Did you make me rent that house on purpose?'

'I don't understand.'

'Did you know Njoku?'

'Baby, I knew him in passing, that house was suggested to me by a friend who is a developer.' He changes the tone of his voice as he says, 'I just got back from my trip. I am in Lagos now, can I come over?'

I stifle the urge to tell him to go hug a naked wire. Instead, I say, 'No, I am busy, and we have—'

'Another time. I will come over, maybe the day after tomorrow.'

I sigh. 'No. Unless you want to end up like Njoku, don't show up at my house again.'

I don't wait for a response before ending the call.

FORTY-TWO

Still

TUESDAY
10.10 a.m.

I steady my trembling hands by clenching the deep ends of the pockets attached to my overalls. The chaos in the police station today mirrors my state of mind. The officer who usually leads me to Juicy is leaning against a pole beside the counter.

'*Oga*, good morning.'

He sees me and immediately looks away.

I inch closer and announce myself loudly. 'Good morning, *sah*!'

He snaps the newspaper shut. 'Madam! Why you *dey* shout for here? This is a place of peace, please!'

'Sorry, *sah*.'

He hisses, 'Follow me.'

He takes me down the same corridor, but then takes a

different turn, leading me to a cell. It is a small, dark room with a rusty gate. The smell of urine hits strongly as I enter into the room. Juicy is there with the DPO. Her legs dangle from the bed she is seated on, and there is a small nylon bag beside her. The DPO turns to me.

'You have thirty minutes. Juicy is being transferred today at three p.m., so I don't want any wahala.' He leaves with the officer, and I move to sit beside Juicy.

'I am sorry. I thought we still had time.'

She stands up and goes to the window. 'I need to get out of here soon. I can't have my baby in this place. I can't.'

What?

FORTY-THREE

Juicy's Confession VI

Like, who gets pregnant by their sugar daddy? Can you imagine what people would say? A sugar daddy they think I killed is now my baby's daddy. Just imagine. It's going to leak somehow. I just know it. People are not great at keeping other people's secrets. You should know. You are writing a whole book on other people's private business.

Anyway, back to my good news. My baby. I thought my womb was damaged, so this baby is a miracle. I don't care who the father is, although I think it is Farouk's, since he is the only one that I sleep with without protection. But I still don't care. I am keeping the baby regardless. It is mine.

I had been feeling funny for two weeks, so after leaving Farouk one morning, days before the brawl, I stopped by a pharmacy on my way to campus. My plan was actually to tell Farouk or Njoku once I could settle down to figure out whose child it was. Logically everything was leaning towards Farouk. I was going to tell him the morning of

Njoku's death, or maybe when I got to Cape Town. I was just looking for the right time.

But then the women called me to come home, and I found Njoku dead. And everything suddenly became too much.

As I saw blood drip from his lifeless body parts, I started to ask myself: What if this man is the father of my child? What should I tell the child? *Your daddy died and I wasn't there because I was with his best friend who was also my sugar daddy?* What kind of life am I setting the child up for? All of these questions were on my mind as the women spoke to me. I just shut down and followed the instructions they gave me.

Now that I have had time to think about it, I realise that I need to get out of here. I'll get a job and raise my child. I have some savings, although my phone, which has all of my bank details on it, was taken away. I still have some money, somewhere. I am not giving up my child nor am I raising my child in prison.

My real name is Obiageli Mbelu. Juicy is an alias I got from one of my sugar daddies who always joked that my punani was juicy and wet. The truth is you are your name. Your name is your identity. I decided to go with Juicy, and it made me very popular. The name Obiageli didn't do a lot for me. Once I changed my name, I started to get messages from the big boys on Snapchat because they all wanted some of my juice.

It is also catchy. I have seen several TikTok videos about

me since I got arrested. A friendly cell mate of mine has been sleeping with one of the police officers, so she has a phone on her. One TikToker titled hers, *The Juice of Juicy's Story*, while another went for, *Juicy Gist about Juicy the Killer.* See what I mean? At least there is something to laugh at in all this.

I told the DPO I was pregnant, and he advised me to abort the baby, he said they have someone who aborts children for offenders. He said, and I quote:

'You will be good as new in two days. They will even wash your stomach and take out all the *yama yama* all the men *don* put inside.'

Just imagine.

I kept quiet as he talked nonsense because I don't have time for foolishness. This baby is for me, and it will go to school and never have to worry about money. I will work hard for my child so he or she can go on to be whatever they want. Whatever the child decides, I will support it. I am not putting pressure on my child to be anything but honest, hardworking and happy.

The moment your book comes out, I will feel a lot better because the world will know my story and someone from those international organisations will help me. Ara, I have so much faith in you. You are my final hope.

FORTY-FOUR

How to Keep a Baby

TUESDAY
11.12 a.m.

After a few moments of silence, I make her an offer.

'If you don't get out on time, I can help you take care of your baby.'

She lifts her head from my right shoulder. 'I thought you said you had found me a lawyer.'

'I did, and he will do his best to get you out. But if he doesn't manage before your due date, that will be our only other option. Don't worry, I'll come here with your baby to see you every week.'

She starts to cry. 'I don't want to leave my baby. Please, Ara. Fix it.'

'I promise you I am doing my best to get you out. The lawyer will come and see you today.'

'But I am getting transferred.'

'No, you are not. I am not going to let that happen.'

FORTY-FIVE

Home Sweet Home

TUESDAY

12.45 p.m.

Once I get onto Osborne Road, I dial Ezu's number.

'Hi, Ezu. Have you looked into that girl's case? I need you to step in today.'

He chuckles. 'Today *ke*? The owners of our firm are a little sceptical about taking her on, Ara.'

'Don't you have your own side practice?'

'I do, but—'

'Ezu, I'll pay your full retainer fee for a year if you go to the station and stop her transfer. Please make sure she doesn't leave that place.' I listen to his soft breaths in the contemplative silence. His retainer fee is two million naira. That's a lot of money in the present economy for a man who has a wife and two young children.

'Okay, Ara, but if I lose my job—'

'You won't. This is Nigeria. Use your guys to represent

her, but you as a lawyer need to get there now and stop the transfer.'

'Now?'

'Yes. I am texting you the address.'

'I have work . . . '

'Ezu, please.'

'Fine. Send the details and then I'll forward an invoice after.'

'Thank you.'

~

The estate gate is open when I get home. I don't see Solomon, which is a good thing. I park and walk up to my house. Little shards of glass in the interlocked pathway catch the sun, glinting in the light. My ribcage cinches tight and my breath comes out like the gasp of someone drowning.

My front door is wide open.

I run in on wobbly legs, feeling like I am losing my mind. Everything in my house is upside down. Even the sofa Rude Victoria once admired has been swung aside and stained. With my breathing coming in short gasps, I head towards the dining area to look for my laptop, typewriter and my notepad.

They are gone.

My weak knees can no longer hold my shocked body up and I lean against the wall to make sense of what I am seeing.

'Hello . . . ' a male voice calls through the open doorway.

Who the fuck is this?

'Good afternoon, Miss Ara Ikoyi?'

With great effort, I pull myself away from the wall and walk to the front door. There's a man standing in a grey suit, holding a black satchel, those ones that hold iPads. He has the pin-sized, glassy eyes and stature of a miniature teddy bear. I've never seen him before.

'Who are you?'

'I am Babajide Taiwo. I am a lawyer representing the owners of this estate. I have a letter for you.'

'Excuse me . . . ?'

He steps into my violated home. 'It's an eviction notice, Madam. You have been given immediate notice to vacate the premises for destroying the property.'

What!

My head spins. Only one thing drops into my mind to do.

'Please, hold on.'

I usher him out of the door and close it. I quickly dial Ezu's number. He cuts me off but sends a text that he is on his way to the police station and can't talk.

Knock knock.

I open the door again. 'Look, Mr Lawyer. I didn't do this,' I explain weakly.

He shakes his head. 'I am sorry. The owner of the house filed a complaint against you this morning, citing destruction to her property. You have a week to leave before the police get involved.'

'Sir, if this is about the house rent increment, I can pay and I am willing—'

'I am not here about that, those that refuse to pay will be evicted after six months of notice. The owner of this house wants you out today for destruction of property. You know her husband just died.'

What is happening?

Her property? Edith really owns this house?

The lawyer watches me quizzically and he looks even more like a cartoon character.

'Madam, I understand you are a writer. I'll advise you to please leave without making a ruckus. They are not asking you to pay damages. They just want you out.'

I start crying. 'Sir, I was robbed. My laptop and my notepad were stolen.'

He rubs at his short, thick eyebrows, then looks at me with pity.

'Ara, I don't know you, but I am asking you to please leave. You can always buy another laptop and even writing paper. My clients are not people to mess with, no matter how successful you are.'

He tucks the letter into my hand and leaves. I close the broken door and head back inside, weeping as I walk up the stairs to my bedroom – which was also ransacked. I lay on the bed anyway, feeling the weight of my world collapsing on my head.

I don't know how much time passes before my phone rings again. I lift it with a heavy hand to look at the screen. Ezu is finally calling me back. I swipe right to answer.

'Ezu?'

When he speaks, his voice struggles to compete with all the noise in the background. 'Ara, how far?! Even though we delayed the transfer today, my team and I will need hard evidence to stop the judge from sending her to Kirikiri next week.'

I wipe my nose and clear my throat. 'How will you get it?' I ask quietly.

'I have a private investigator, but I'll also need your help. Do you have anything that can help me? She is your neighbour after all.'

'I just found out about the girl two weeks ago, Ezu.'

'Oh, so you don't have anything—'

'I don't, but—'

'Juicy says she spoke to you, and you know some people—'

What do I do? Do I tell him I know the killers? If they can steal my laptop, evict me on a Tuesday, find out about my son, what more are these insane women willing to do?

'Ezu, I'll send you an email tomorrow with what I know. I have stuff to do today.'

'Okay. I'll get my guys on it.'

I end the call and walk over to my closet, flinging it open. *These people are not playing.* I have no plans to report my missing laptop and manuscript to the police. They probably have it in their custody. I asked them what would happen if I didn't stop.

Now I know.

~

When my head clears, I remember the recorder. I do have evidence, something Ezu might be able to use, but I am too scared to hand it over. Who knows who they would hurt if it got in his hands?

With my bags packed. I sit downstairs on the two-seater for some time to email Ezu. I attach some of the recordings that my phone can tap from the recorder, but not all of them. I can't tell him everything, but I can give him clues.

Hey Ezu,

How are you? I have attached some information that might help you. The girl is not a killer. I have sent you some money as well. Please acknowledge receipt.

From the recordings, you will discover that Juicy is pregnant, so I need you to get this case wrapped before she gives birth.

Talk soon,

Ara

Before I toss my phone, an email from Susan comes through.

Hi Ara,

Waving at you from a rainy New York City.

So, I have some exciting news . . . Due to the success of your first three books, we have a new three-book deal from your UK/US publishers. I'll be in touch once I've had a chance to discuss it with them in detail.

I look forward to reading the first hundred pages of your next story. I know this will be another bestseller.

Best,

Susan

Three-book offer? When all of my notes, ideas for future books and manuscript have just been stolen?

I put my phone away, pick up my handbag and carry the luggage over to my car. I can see Long Legs watching me through her window, arms akimbo and half naked. Just then, a text comes in from Dotun:

Hey Boo,

The film rights contract has been amended per request and the updated version has been signed. First tranche of payment has come in, and we have forwarded your cut to you. You should receive it in another day or two. They will send us a schedule for you and options for writers/showrunners in the coming months. Congratulations, baby girl. I am incredibly proud of you.

SUBMIT YOUR MANUSCRIPT!

As I drive out of House Twenty-One Estate with the windows down, I feel the wind drying the tears on my face. On the expressway that leads towards Falomo, I see a billboard with Mr Nicholas's face on it, advising people to rent at affordable prices on the Island from him. One of the addresses on the billboard is House Twenty-One Estate. Will I ever understand the connection between him, Njoku and Yele? Who was I really paying rent to all this while, Njoku or Nicholas? Or Yele? I wonder how many more men own estates on the island where they keep their sugar babies, side chicks and mistresses. I wonder how many more murders it will take for the sickness to stop.

Unwelcome eyes always stay too long on a beautiful woman.

The only crime Juicy ever committed was being born beautiful. Beautiful and poor. Words that should never be in the same sentence in a country like Nigeria.

For me, my crime was being born unwanted. The only thing that has ever loved me is my writing/my art. Not even Vincent, Godsword or Yele. These women and I are the same. We are all fighting battles – the battle of being Nigerian and female. We are looking for freedom.

I know murder is not a way to freedom for a woman. Neither is relying on other people and their assets.

Perhaps it is time for me to buy my own house. I can move to the place where bananas have an Island to themselves.

Or do I flee the motherland for colder pastures?

Wait.

Why is my car making strange sounds? Was that my left tyre that just rolled out and down the street?

Oh fuck!

FORTY-SIX

After

The first thing I smell is antiseptics. It crowds my nostrils and lungs and turns my stomach. I heave, and try to stand up, when a voice calls out:

'Oh, thank heavens, she is awake!!! Nurse, nurse!'

At first, I think I'm dreaming because the person speaking sounds like a character from a Jane Austen movie adaptation. His strong hands hold my shoulders and the smell of mint and coconut aftershave on him dispel the *Izal* I smelled before. Despite the ringing in my ears, I force myself to speak, an oversized lump stings my throat as the words form.

'What happened?'

'You were in an accident, ma'am. Your car hit a parked bus.' The man speaking is as black as me, just another probable returnee. 'No one died, don't worry. You are very lucky. The doctors say you only suffered a slight concussion. You are in Military Hospital Ikoyi. I brought you here after I witnessed what happened.'

He waves my phone at me. 'Do you have someone you can call?'

'Dotun . . . please call a Dotun on my phone,' I reply.

'What is your pin?'

'1995.'

Suddenly my head starts to spin, so I close my eyes to slow the pace.

~

You know how, in the movies, a person at their moment of death sees a reel of all the key moments in their life before they go to the great beyond? Something like that happens to me as my head spins, except this time, it feels like the universe parts a light curtain that allows a rush of images from the future to suffuse my mind and memory.

The first scene opens with me reworking Juicy's story after I have gotten the back-up file from my email. Other scenes follow. I see Ezu and I fighting for Juicy in every way possible. I see her beautiful baby and watch as justice is served. The climax of the movie is where I go to look for Deleayo in Ogbomosho, finding ways to reunite with him – wherever he is.

The final scene is an omniscient view of the readers once the book is published – watching them see Juicy's story with fresh eyes and understanding that behind every secret is a story. Of hope and despair. Of loss and pain. Of strangeness and uncommon valour.

Of freedom.

FORTY-SEVEN

The Beginning

EIGHTEEN MONTHS LATER

1.00 p.m.

They are seated in the front row – Deleayo with his parents, Juicy with her baby and the man I now call husband. They all look like different pieces of many unrelated puzzles that I have somehow managed to make fit. Down the aisle, Dotun leans against the door of Rovingheights bookstore looking like a proud mother over the small crowd that has gathered for the reading of my new book.

As the reading goes on, Ezu sneaks in silently and Juicy waves him to sit beside her.

'Ara, is it true that this book is based on true-life events?' A voice from the audience calls me back to them.

'Hmmm, you know I can't reveal my sources, and I don't want to get sued.' I respond. Laughter cascades through the middle of the room. 'I can however say if this was based on real life, every single character in the book got exactly what they deserved and that is all that matters to me.'

The crowd scatters into smaller groups waiting to get their copies signed.

I catch a glimpse of my newly found family in the corner, waiting as I scribble my signature on the books.

Slowly, it dawns on me as I take it all in that life that Juicy and I are no longer alone.

We have each other.

We have our children.

We have You.

ACKNOWLEDGEMENTS

Let's take a moment to appreciate the Lord for helping me write my third book! Look at God!!

I wrote Ara/Bawarin and Juicy/Obiageli thinking of my mother and the late Professor Foluke Ogunleye – women who took the hard road to become teachers. I thank Juicy, Ara and the women in House Twenty-One who allowed me to be a tenant in the estate as I wrote. I salute them too, for the secrets they keep, for it can *never* be me.

There are so many things in my life that inspired the direction of this story. One of the most important is a television programme I grew up watching on LTV 8 called *Ah! Nkan Be* – a programme that told the most unbelievable stories of things people go through in life. As a young girl, I often wondered why anyone had to be wrung so thoroughly by the hands of fate. This book is the adult version of that little girl trying to answer that question.

On that note, I would like to thank the amazing people who have lifted me up and made me a better person:

Captain, Dunni, Eniola, my beautiful nieces and handsome nephews: I am grateful for you. I love you all so much.

Professor Olorode: I look forward to discussing everything in this book with you. I am still waiting on the write-up for *Nearly all the Men in Lagos are Mad* and *Only Big Bumbum Matters Tomorrow*, sir. Whiny Whipsy loves you very much.

Uche Nwokedi: Uncle, are you really gone? Are we no longer going to take it one day at a time? You gave me a stage when no one would, you got me out of a contract, and you never stopped believing in me. Thank you, sir. If there is a library in heaven, I hope you read this and know I loved you deeply. I will now attach myself to Aunty Winifred because how else will I atone for the years of silence? I really thought we had time. *Sun re o.*

Obafemi Awolowo University: While I was in school, I didn't understand the Student Union body. They disrupted everything and I was tired of the endless strikes. Now that I am grown, I know that if you don't fight for what you believe in, then you stand for nothing. So, I am thankful for OAU, the school that sparked the fighting spirit in me.

Writing Companions: Many thanks to Chimeka Garricks, who held my hands when I first started writing, I am forever a fan. Chimamanda Ngozi Adichie stoked this fire in me with *Half of a Yellow Sun* so I thank all the authors that have beamed a light onto my path with their books. I thank

Tahirah Avosuahi, Molly Crawford, Charlotte Seymour, and Seun, the people who bore all the pressure as we made sense of my words on paper. Thank you all for making me a MUCH better storyteller.

Tobi Eyinade and her team: Thank you all so much for your hard work on my books. Tobi, please know I am a huge fan of everything you do.

My social media family: My very loyal readers and followers on TikTok, X, Facebook and Instagram are responsible for my incredible global growth as a creative and writer. Thank you for making me feel seen and making this career everything.

My team: Many thanks to my entire publishing team in America, UK, South Africa, East Africa, West Africa and the agency for always going on these wild rides with me. I am a better storyteller because of YOU. I send you all my gratitude wrapped in ribbons.

Book clubs/Bookstores: I don't think anyone would know who I am without the immense support of all the bookstores and clubs in Africa and the world. So, I thank them for the platform.

My mother: *Abake mi atata, my friend, and my sister kare iya mi.* We are on this journey together. Let's keep going with GOD leading us. Thank you for buying me those books growing up. Thank you for holding my hands on the days I couldn't lift them so that I kept writing. Thank you for supporting me with everything. You know how much I love you.

Thank you, LORD. You are the pen that never runs dry. I am humbled by your presence. *E seun Baba mi Agba.* You are my love, and my everything, I bow at your feet forever and always. Thank you for telling me this story. I hope my words carried it well on paper.

Read on for a sneak peek of Damilare's bold, funny and profound novel.

Available now

PROLOGUE

“I plan to renovate my bumbum in Lagos, live there for some time, and hopefully meet the love of my life!”

You had hoped your clever use of the word “renovate” would douse the tension in the room, elicit a smile from those assembled, perhaps even fits of laughter. Instead, you saw your mother digging her big toe into the old living room rug, the red nail paint chipping as she dug deeper.

Silence.

“Ehn? Témì, ṣé o ti bẹ̀rẹ̀ sí í mu igbó ni? Have you started smoking weed? Why would you do that?” Aunty Jummai barked at you while retying her wrapper. The smoke from the jollof rice cooking in the kitchen caused her eyes to water.

A ringtone was hastily silenced; someone muffled a cough. The lawyer who had been getting ready to take his leave sank deeper into the chair your father had loved.

“No, Aunty. Smoking kills. Would I fix my buttocks if I wanted to die young? I am doing it because I want to—it’s my body,” you answered as truthfully as you could.

Now you were stuck in the house, with no chance of fleeing

the slow fire that was burning within your family. You were unlikely to make the consultation scheduled for ten days' time.

Nigerian families can be an obstacle in a girl's journey to a figure eight.

part one

TODAY, THIS SMALL YANSH MUST GO!

TÉMÌ IS A BLACKBOARD

Your bumbum has always been flat.

You stared, as usual, hoping that some fat had miraculously found its way into it. In your midi midnight-blue lace dress, you looked at your slender frame in the full-length mirror that stood next to your bed. You lifted one hand to clutch both breasts and touched the small of your back with the other. If only your ass was bigger, your tiny waist would have been a magnet for compliments. You dropped both hands and sighed. This was your morning ritual. For yourself. For your sanity. For your sense of somebodiness.

You looked at the window opposite your bed and made a mental note to dust it and wash the curtains that hung loosely by its sides.

You thought about what you planned to do. You thought about your family.

You sighed again.

How do you inform your family members that you intend to surgically enlarge your buttocks without receiving a barrage of curses? How do you slip it into a conversation with Màámi that you intend to relocate to Lagos to meet the man who will love you senseless? How do you tell your older sister, who, until a week ago, you hadn't seen in five years, that you are hoping to stay in her Lagos apartment while you recover from surgery, maybe even stay a few more months? How?

These questions had been nagging at you since you decided to take the big step to redeem your backside. Time was not your friend; you needed to make the announcement quickly if you were to cash in on the new Easter discount you had seen on Instagram yesterday. The advertisement was clear and straight to the point:

Laydiz, this is for you!

This offer lasts till the end of the month.

So if you really want to enter Easter with a snatched body,

now is the time to go for it.

For my slim laydiz, BBL is possible!

For my thick laydiz, BBL is possible!

Fillers, BBL, nonsurgical butt lift . . . this clinic has got you!

Don't go to where they will not shape your yansh well o.